DESERT FIRE

MARCIA LYNN McCLURE

Published by Distractions Ink
P.O. Box 15971
Rio Rancho, NM 87174

©Copyright 2007, 2011 by M. L. Meyers
A.K.A. Marcia Lynn McClure
Cover Photography by
©Rod Stegmann | Dreamstime.com
Cover Design by
Sheri L. Brady | MightyPhoenixDesignStudio.com

Second Printed Edition: 2011

McClure, Marcia Lynn, 1965—
Desert Fire: a novella/by Marcia Lynn McClure.

ISBN 978-0-9838074-3-8

Library of Congress Control Number: 2011933850

Printed in the United States of America

To Dixie,
Ahhh, the memories!
Walks and wagons…mailboxes and homemade bread.
The White Ranger and Wind in His Throat…firecrackers
and egg hairstyles.
Thank you for being a central piece of my heart…
A nurturer to my soul…
And my treasured friend.

CHAPTER ONE

She felt something on her face. It was cool, soothing, moist. Her throat burned and constricted and when she tried to swallow, she couldn't.

"Ma'am?" She heard the voice, but it seemed so far away. "Ma'am?" It came again, closer this time. "Can you hear me, ma'am?" A man's voice, deep and stern.

She attempted to speak, but found it impossible. She tried to nod in response, but her head was pounding like a drum was pinned up inside it.

"Open your eyes if you can. Open 'em," the voice insisted.

She opened her eyes just a slit and quickly clenched them shut again as searing rays of sunlight burned through her. She sensed movement and the demanding voice came once more.

"Now...try again."

It was a voice not to be ignored. She tried to lift her hand to shade her face, but her own body would not obey her mind's command. She opened her eyes slightly and when the sun didn't blind her painfully again, she was able to open them completely. Everything was blurry for several seconds but she could make out a dark figure bending over her.

"Can you see?" the voice asked firmly.

She blinked several times clearing her vision slightly.

"Yes," she mouthed, though no sound escaped her blistered lips. A hand slipped beneath her head and lifted it.

"Here...keep still and let this stay on your tongue for a minute," the voice said, and she felt the first cool, life giving drops of water moisten her mouth. She couldn't move her tongue at first, but the second time the stranger offered the water from the canteen, she was able to swallow it.

After several mouthfuls of water she felt more alert and realized her face, arms and shoulders felt tight and hot.

"Now...what's your name, girl? And how'd ya' end up out here?" the man asked.

She could see clearly then and for the first time she looked up into the face that belonged to the voice.

"I don't know," she answered in a forced whisper.

The man let out a sigh, tipped his hat back on his head and looked around with an expression of both bewilderment and annoyance.

"You don't know how you ended up lyin' out in the middle of nowhere, with nothin' or no one with you?" he asked, still looking around.

"No," she whispered, feeling suddenly terrified at the realization.

The stranger stood up and pulled his hat down into place again.

"Well...I guess I'll just haul ya' on home and we'll think on it from there." He walked over to a nearby tree and untied a horse. "Come on Bill. Ma will love this," he muttered.

The man led the horse to where she was lying and she sat up more terrified still.

"I can't possibly go with you, sir!" she whispered as loud as possible.

He smiled and chuckled. "Well, sweetheart... what do you plan on doin'? Feedin' the coyotes?" He hunkered down looking directly into her face. "Or... there are all kinds of worse things you could feed..." Then his smile turned into a frown as he looked at the ground around her. "Do you feel anything crawlin' on you anywhere, girl?"

She thought it an odd question but answered, "No."

He pulled her up until she was sitting straight and began running his hand over her back and through her hair. She realized that her shirtwaist was torn because she could feel his hands on the exposed skin of her shoulders. She gasped as she looked down and saw that it was also torn in front and gaped open exposing her entire collarbone.

As the frown on his face intensified the man quickly ran his hand over her back once more then moved to her waist. She instinctively moved to slap him, but he caught her hand and looked angrily into her face.

"I ain't out for a good time, sweetheart," he growled

through clenched teeth. He pushed her back down and she wanted to weep when he lifted up her skirts and began feeling her right leg. But her state of severe dehydration prevented any tears from even developing.

"Well, you certainly ain't from around here," the man stated as he unfastened her bustle throwing it aside. "Women don't bother too much with these contraptions 'round these parts." Then he stopped. "Don't move," he commanded and she obeyed as she felt something crawling on her flesh under the left leg of her pantaloons.

She watched with utter mortification as the stranger's hand slowly slid beneath the cloth of her pantaloons and toward her knee. His hand clamped around something and he quickly withdrew it.

"Sorry little cuss!" he mumbled as he threw something to the ground and drew a large knife from his boot.

She then witnessed him smashing a large, sandy colored scorpion into the dirt with his well-worn boot. When she looked up again it was in time to see him cut the palm of his hand with the knife and begin sucking on the wound. He did this several times, spitting his own blood from his mouth each time.

"That sorry little cuss stung me," he mumbled. "They don't usually kill you, unless you're allergic or somethin'. But they make you awful sick and the sting gets terrible sore." He looked at her oddly for a moment. "You feel like you're gonna faint or somethin'?" he asked.

She swallowed hard and shook her head to dispel the

awful dizziness in it. The man slipped the knife back into his boot and pulled her up to a sitting position again.

"Well, least you had sense enough to nearly drop dead 'round here," he muttered.

She watched as he pulled an odd shaped plant from the ground and broke open a few of the strange looking leaves. He squeezed out a slimy substance and began to apply it to her face. It smelled unpleasant, but felt very cool and soothing.

When he finished, he wiped his hand on his dusty trousers and said, "Now, let's see if you can sit a horse."

He pulled her to her feet, but her knees buckled and her mind began swimming. He caught her and sat her down again.

"I'm sorry," she whispered, wishing she could cry.

"Hang on there a minute," he said, with a hint more of kindness in his voice.

She watched, perfectly alarmed, as he actually proceeded to remove his shirt and wet it with water from the canteen. Even more disgraceful was the fact that he wore no form of undergarment beneath! None whatsoever! He was standing there bare from the waist up! And judging from the bronze color of his torso, he paraded around in such a state often.

When he looked at her again she covered her eyes with her sore hands.

He chuckled. "I believe you're blushin' under that sunburn, girl. You're definitely from somewhere else."

He draped the wet shirt over her head and shoulders

and pulled her to her feet yet again. She still needed a great deal of support to stand. She tried to push herself away when her hands touched his bare chest as they searched for support.

"Tarnation, girl," he grumbled, taking her hands in his. "This is no time for propriety." She thought the word sounded a little out of character with his odd, rather Southern sounding accent.

He proceeded to run her hands from his shoulders slowly down and over his solid stomach. "See don't feel any different than your baby brother. You must be an unmarried one as well." He steadied her again. "Now, let's get you home to Mama so she can see the damage." He then lifted her onto the horse which sneezed and stomped his foreleg several times.

"Settle down, Bill. She's with me." He mounted behind her and pulled her tightly against his body. "Try not to fall off...it ain't far."

She was still too shocked by her recent lesson in anatomy to take much notice of the shameful way she sat astride the horse. But, somehow she knew, that until that moment, she had always ridden sidesaddle. A great wave of fatigue was overtaking her and she couldn't help but let her head fall back against his shoulder.

"I'm sorry," she whispered. "I think I'm going to faint." She felt his arm tighten around her waist and the heat of his breath on her face as he spoke in her ear.

"It ain't far, girl. Now listen here, I'm Jackson McCall. This here feller you're on is Bill. He don't care much for nobody but me...so you sit real still and hang on tight."

She could smell leather, bacon, and perspiration... but it was somehow a pleasant and comforting combination. "Yes, sir," she whispered, trying to keep her eyes open.

"Yes, sir?" he repeated in an astonished whisper. "Where are you from, girl?"

She tried and tried to pull an answer from her fevered brain. But she truly couldn't.

"I don't know," she whispered, just before she gave into the need to be unconscious.

CHAPTER TWO

"I think she's comin' around, Mary. Close the curtains... her eyes should be mighty sensitive yet." A soft feminine voice was drifting into her dreams and she fought the urge to wake up from them.

She was dreaming of the handsomest man she had ever seen. One of those rugged types that lived in the savage West that she had read about. His body was darkened from hours in the sun, brown hair lightened by the same hours in the sun, square jaw badly in need of a close shave. Perfectly shaped lips and nose, straight teeth whiter than white, and intense green eyes shaded by long dark lashes. He had rescued her from something, though she couldn't think what.

"Wake up, honey. Can you hear us? Oh, Mary, I do hope she's well." The dream swept away as awakening triumphed.

She opened her eyes and blinked several times. They felt dry and hot. When her vision cleared she beheld two women hovering over her. One was an older woman, perhaps fifty, and the other was young, eighteen maybe. Both were smiling down at her kindly.

"Well! Finally!" the elder woman exclaimed. "We were beginning to wonder if we should send for a doctor."

"Where am I?" the still recovering girl asked the two women at her bedside.

The older woman answered, "You're at the McCall ranch. We're near Cortez, Colorado. I'm Maggie McCall and this is Mary Henderson, one of our dear neighbors. What's your name, dear?"

Tears began to trickle from the corners of the girl's eyes, leaving moisture across her temples.

"I don't know. I really can't remember. It's so frightening," she sobbed.

Mary dabbed at the tears with a handkerchief. "Now, now. It's all right. It'll all come back to you in time. Meanwhile, you're with the best people in the world and I could use someone near my own age around here. Jackson told us that you seemed to have lost your mind...um...memory...but we were hopin' that some rest would help."

"Let's get you all bathed and freshened up and you'll feel much better, sweety," Maggie said. "Let's see...what would you like us to call you...how about Annie? I always wanted a daughter named Annie. How's that? Just until you remember your own name," she added.

'Annie' smiled and nodded. "It's lovely," she encouraged the kind woman smiling down at her.

"Mary, go tell Baker to bring the wash tub in here so we can have some privacy, would you?" Maggie said, helping Annie to sit up.

Mary nodded and left. Maggie sat down on the foot of the bed, smoothed her apron a bit and began chatting. Annie knew that she was trying to help her to feel comfortable and it was working.

"Well, a little about us. I'm Maggie McCall and I've got me three beautiful little boys. Their daddy, Colonel Robert Jackson McCall was the love of my life and the handsomest man on this earth. He passed three years back and it hasn't been easy on us. We miss him more than anythin'. We came here after the war and started ranchin' and loved it. My boys are hard workin' gentlemen...even if I can't get their grammar the way I would like it. The oldest is Jackson...then Baker and then Matt. They're just itchin' for you to wake up. When Jackson rode up two days ago with you on Bill...I nearly dropped my teeth!"

"Two days ago!" Annie interrupted.

"Yes, dear. You've been in here with a fever and restin' for over two days," Maggie explained, looking concerned. "We all took turns the first two nights sittin' with you for fear you'd quit on us. Your skin is lookin' so much better! It's almost completely peeled off now and I'm sure that feels nicer to you."

There was a knock on the door and when Maggie said, 'Come in,' a tall, very handsome young man that Annie judged to be in his early twenties, entered carrying a large metal tub. He looked familiar to her somehow when he smiled, removed his hat and offered her his hand.

"Baker McCall, ma'am. Glad to see you feelin'

11

better." His smile was radiant and she smiled back as he shook her hand instead of kissing it as she had expected for some reason. He nodded, kissed his mother's cheek, winked at Mary and left the room.

"I'll bring in the water, Mrs. McCall," Mary said and left also.

"Baker. Your middle son, Mrs. McCall? He's so very tall!" Annie commented as Maggie helped her stand.

"Oh my, yes! All my boys are tall as redwoods. Though Baker is the tallest. Six feet three inches he is... even! And call me, Maggie, please." Then she went on.

"Jackson says you must be from back east...says you kept calling him 'sir' and were near to dyin' of embarrassment when he was checkin' you for critters. And a bustle, even! I never could understand why a woman would want to make her backside look bigger! Mine's big enough on its own."

Annie giggled. Everything felt good here. The air was dry and there was a cool breeze coming through the window.

After Mary had filled the tub with warmed water, the two ladies left and Annie soaked for a long time before getting out and dressing in the calico dress that Maggie had laid out for her. She sensed that she had never worn anything quite so simple and comfortable, though she felt a little under dressed without a sturdier corset.

Maggie knocked on the door and Annie asked her to come in.

"My! You do look like you feel better, dear. May I

do your hair? My fingers are just itchin' to work with that mane of yours." Annie smiled and let Maggie braid her hair.

Maggie marveled at the lovely hair on their nameless guest. It was long, thick and so black that it seemed to hold blue light. This girl's eyes were an unusually light shade of blue and flattered by thick black lashes. Her mouth was perfect and still held the lovely natural wine color of youth. In fact, the girl was physically perfect in every respect. Maggie had also noticed an unusual grace possessed by the girl. Even her simplest movements were lovely.

"What do you think, dear?" Maggie asked as she finished.

Annie looked in the mirror and studied the long French braid. It was so divinely simple! She loved it. Her attention was drawn to the reflection of her face. She frowned for a moment not really recognizing herself.

"Who am I, Mrs. McCall?" She felt hot stinging tears begin to fill her eyes. Maggie reached out, turning her and facing her sternly.

"Now, don't get discouraged, dear. It'll all come back to you...and even if it doesn't...you've got us now."

Annie smiled and the tears escaped her eyes. "I can't just live here forever, Mrs. McCall! You don't even know who I am? What if I'm a murderess...a criminal... what if..." she cried.

"Now, you stop that. That couldn't be. You're too nice a girl. Don't be worryin' about it. I'm sure you're no murderer." Maggie smiled. "Now, come on out for dinner. The boys will be in any minute bellerin' for food."

Maggie took Annie's hand and led her out into the brightest looking room the girl had ever been in. Even though she had no memories to draw upon, she knew she had never been in a cheerier room. The walls were brightly whitewashed and there were three windows through which the evening sunshine poured. Jars and jars of freshly canned peaches lined one counter and their sweet aroma still lingered heavily in the air. The curtains were red checked as was the tablecloth on the table in the center of the room. Annie smiled from the pure delight that it sent through her. This was a home! Not just a house with a mother and her three sons. A real home.

Baker was the first one through the squeaky screen door.

"Mama! That ol' Root tore up the north fence again! I am sick and tired of chasin' down that ol' ornery bull. I gotta tug myself to death on that ring to get him to stop. I tell you his nose is made of steel...'cause tuggin' on that ring in it don't slow him down one lick," he said with a frown. He looked over at Annie. "Well, good evenin' to you, miss. You're as pretty as apple blossoms in spring time," he said, his frown turning to a radiant smile.

Annie returned the greeting with her own fascinating

smile. "And you've been taught well the art of flattery, Mr. McCall, sir."

"Weren't taught, ma'am. Got it from my daddy. Purely natural."

"Don't let him fool you, miss. He works hard at it. I got all the natural good looks and talent." Another tall, handsome young man had entered the room through the door. He smiled slyly, took Annie's hand, bent and kissed it lightly on the back. "Matthew Robert McCall, miss. And I'm right pleased to see that you're up and about and lookin' so very lovely."

Annie giggled softly with delight. Never had she seen two more attractive men in all her life! Not only handsome, both had brown hair and brown eyes, and were tall and boiling over with personality. Something told her that it took an overwhelming amount of positive personality to make people feel the way she did just then. The door squeaked again and another man entered the room.

"Now, that…that there is our big brother, Jackson. He weren't endowed with nothin' but a mean streak. He's a smart mouthed tease, and he works too much and too hard to be good for any feller," Baker teased.

Jackson McCall's eyes captured Annie's. Something about his very presence was overwhelming and Annie couldn't help but take a step backward when he approached and offered her his hand. His was the face she'd seen in her dream, and a vision of him standing before her bare from the waist up flashed through her mind and she went crimson. He reached out and took her hand, shaking it twice, very ceremoniously.

"Glad to see you're up and about, miss. I wasn't too sure myself that we found you in time. And don't listen to my brothers. I'm the handsomest and the smartest! The spittin' image of my daddy."

Somewhere Annie found her composure. "I thank you, sir, for finding me and bringing me here. I surely would've perished if you hadn't."

The three brothers looked back and forth at one another with raised eyebrows, then back to Annie.

"Darlin'…I hope you'll loosen up a bit around us boys. You're too polite. Now, what do we call you?" Baker asked.

"She let me pick a name for her boys," Mrs. McCall chirped, smiling proudly. The three men looked at their mother. "I've decided on, Annie," she announced, beaming.

"Annie!" came the simultaneous exclamation from all three.

"For Pete's sake, Mama! We've had three cows and an old sow named Annie," Jackson grumbled.

"Well, now we have a beautiful girl in our home named Annie. And I'm sure she's starving." She helped Annie sit down in one of the chairs at the table and Baker and Matt sat on either side of her with Jackson, Mary and herself across from them.

Matt leaned over and whispered, "Mama always wanted a daughter named Annie so bad that everything that come along stock wise that was female, she named

Annie. It's really a compliment you see...to be named after three cows and a sow."

Annie smiled. She felt safe. For the moment. But something in the back of her mind was nagging at her sense of security. How she wished she could remember.

Never had Annie tasted such delicious food! She was convinced Mrs. McCall was truly a culinary expert. After dinner everyone retired to the front of the house. A refreshing breeze filled the room and it was comforting to sit and listen to the family's conversation about the day.

"You know, ol' Buck Woodly is sellin' that bull of his, Mama," Baker began. "He wants a piece for him, but I'm willin' to buy him myself if we can get rid of ol' Root."

"Ol' Root isn't any more difficult than any other bull, Baker. He just has it in for you," Maggie said.

"That's right, Baker," Matt added. "You never shoulda done his tail that way three years ago. He remembers. Don't think he doesn't."

"He don't act up with me or Matt," Jackson said, smiling slyly at his brother.

"Well, fine then. Fine. You boys run along side him a yankin' on that ring in his nose from now on. I'm tired of the ol' cuss," Baker added.

"He has a ring in his nose?" Annie asked out loud without thinking.

Everyone in the room looked at her, mouths gaping open as if she bore a ring in her nose.

"You ever seen a bull up close before, Annie?" Mary asked.

"I don't think I have, actually," she said, feeling ridiculous for letting such a question slip from her thoughts and out through her mouth.

"Well, I'll take you out to meet ol' Root tomorrow. And you can tug on his ring a bit if you want. Maybe you can start runnin' him down for me," Baker chuckled, smiling drowsily.

"Mary's comin' over tomorrow to help finish up my peaches, Annie. It'll go so much faster havin' you here to help now," Maggie said, smiling excitedly.

"Oh my, yes! I better be gettin' home, Mrs. McCall. It's late. I'll be here first thing though," Mary said standing.

"I'll take you, Mary," Jackson said, yawning as he stood and headed toward the door. Mary followed.

Annie was horrified. "Aren't you going Mrs. McCall?" she asked frantically.

"Maggie please, dear," Mrs. McCall answered. "Whatever for?" she added lightly.

Everyone in the room was waiting for Annie's answer. She felt silly again, but every logical nerve in her body told her that a woman always had an escort with her when she was with a man.

Jackson answered for her, "Mama, I think she means why aren't you goin' to make sure I don't misbehave. Isn't that right, Annie?" Annie nodded and he smiled slyly at her. "You're definitely not from around these parts, girl. I'm just makin' sure she gets safely home. Nothin' else."

Annie felt a little annoyed at his mocking tone of voice.

"Don't worry, Annie," Mary said smiling. "You'll get used to everything right soon. I'll see you all tomorrow." And they left, unescorted.

❧

Jackson returned later with a crate full of canned pears. "Mary's mama says she'll swap you three dozen quarts of pears for three of peaches, Mama."

Maggie stood up and clapped her hands. "Oh! I was hopin' so. Aren't they lovely, Annie?" she asked.

"Jack," Baker began, "do you think we oughta tell someone that you found Annie?" He seemed so serious that a chill ran down Annie's spine as he asked the question.

Jackson shot a quick look at her and then looking at his mama said, "No."

No one questioned him, but once again Annie's own questioning thoughts came bursting out.

"Why not?" she ventured.

Everyone in the room looked at each other for a moment and then Maggie answered.

"Well, honey...now don't you be worryin' about it... but Jackson thinks maybe we should wait and see if someone is lookin' for you first. Girls just don't end up out in the middle of nowhere lookin' like they were runnin' from somethin'."

Annie looked at Jackson and the serious expression

19

on his face made her shiver involuntarily.

"Why do you think I'm running from something?" she asked directly and so strongly that she was even a little surprised herself.

He answered her bluntly. "You were either dumped there on purpose...or you were runnin' from somethin'. I rode all over that area...didn't find no carpetbag, trunk, clothes lyin' around, and no hand bag. Nothin' that would lead me to think there was some kind of accident that you just wandered off from. I checked with Sheriff Braddock in town, too. No one has come lookin' for a lost girl. You're either runnin' or someone didn't want you around any more."

Baker let out a long sigh. "Boy. You sure is a sweet talker, Jackson. Ain't no one can soften the blow of disturbin' news like you can."

Annie ripped her gaze away from Jackson's unsympathetic one and looked to Baker.

He flashed a dazzling smile and said, "Don't worry about it, Annie. We'll all take good care of you and you're a blessin' for Mama. You ain't got nothin' to worry about. Even good ol' smooth talkin' Jackson won't let nothin' happen to you. He brung you home, didn't he?"

She looked to Maggie and the woman seemed to read her mind. "Now stop that, darlin'! You hear me? You're not a criminal. We're sure of that. So don't even think that way. In fact, Jackson thinks you're probably from a right good family. And that's one reason we'll wait to see if anyone comes lookin' for you."

Annie looked back to Jackson. His eyes seared hers as they met again.

"Why do you think that I'm from a good family?" she asked.

"The way you were dressed. Fancy. And your skin is too...too…pampered for you to have been workin' outside for any amount of time. Especially your hands. Soft as silk. They haven't been workin' hard lately. Look at them fingernails! Ain't a workin' woman on this earth that has fingernails as long as that...all perfectly shaped."

Annie felt like bursting into tears. He seemed so disapproving! Shouldn't a girl be as soft and as feminine as possible?

"Mark another one up for Mr. Subtle, Mama," Baker groaned disgustedly.

"Well, I think it's time we all turned in," Maggie suggested, taking Annie's hand reassuringly.

"Yep. I'm sure ol' Root will be out and about at the crack of dawn," Baker agreed, standing up and stretching. "Where is your mind off to, little brother?" he asked Matt.

Annie noticed that Matt hadn't said a word nearly the whole evening.

"Just thinkin'," he mumbled.

"You think too awful much," Jackson grumbled before leaving the room.

Maggie took Annie back into the bedroom where she had awakened earlier.

"Now, there's some clean nightdresses in here for

you and another dress. We wear 'em out quick here. Don't have time or need of a lot of fancy wear. You get a good night's sleep and don't worry about a thing. Everythin' will come back to you when you're ready. I'll leave the lamp burnin' all night if you like. The hitchin' post is right straight out the back door a ways if you should need it."

Annie frowned. "The hitching post?" she repeated, completely baffled.

Maggie chuckled. "The outhouse, honey. I'll leave you be now. Goodnight...and in the mornin' we'll put up a heap a peaches. Maybe do some preserves as well."

She kissed Annie lightly on the forehead and turned to leave.

"I'm sorry, Mrs. McCall...for the inconvenience. I just don't know what else to do or where else I should go. Maybe we should let the sheriff know that you found me. Surely that would be best."

Maggie put a soft, warm hand on the girl's cheek. "Trust Jackson, Annie. He can be mighty severe at times, but we've all learned that he has a special gift for figurin' things like this out. It's a little unnervin', but if he thinks it's best that we keep you to ourselves for now...then it's best. Now, get some sleep. Think about apple blossoms and rainbows, darlin'."

CHAPTER THREE

The smell was so strong and familiar. Yet she seemed to be having trouble breathing. The air felt heavy and wet. She stood in a grove of enormous black barked trees. They were very beautiful, but sent fear and anxiety riveting through her. What was the familiar odor in the air? She couldn't identify it, but it seemed as familiar to her as breathing itself.

Suddenly then, she knew true terror! The need to flee! To run! Anywhere! She had to escape! From what? She didn't know. Just that she had to get away!

"Help me!" she tried to scream. Over and over she tried, but no sound would escape her throat into the nightmare. "Please, help me!" she cried out. She began to gasp with panic. "Help me!"

"Wake up!" she heard him say. "Wake up. Annie. You're dreamin'. Listen here. You're dreamin'." It was Jackson's commanding voice and she opened her eyes to find her chin held tightly in one of his strong hands.

"You're dreamin', girl. That's all." His face softened for a moment and he smiled ever so slightly at her. "You're fine. Tell me what you were dreamin'."

Annie looked over at Maggie who was smoothing the perspiration from her brow and smiling.

Maggie nodded and mouthed, "Tell him."

She looked back into the eyes of Jackson McCall. They were so disconcerting! She glanced the other way as she spoke.

"I had to run. I couldn't breathe. The air felt so heavy! I could smell something...I know what it is... but I can't remember...and there were enormous trees. Black...oaks...I don't know how I know that. I had to run...and no one would help me. There was no one there to help me."

Annie let the tears trickle down her face. She didn't care if they thought her weak.

Maggie smoothed her hair back. "It's over now, darlin'. You go back to sleep. You need to rest."

"Oh, no! I can't! I don't want to go back to sleep." Annie pleaded, sitting up in bed as fright gripped her.

Jackson stood and Annie's panic was abruptly interrupted as she noticed his lack of attire. He wore no shirt...only red flannels that had been cut away at the waist and made to tie with a string.

Maggie laughed as Jackson turned around to leave and Annie clamped her hands over her eyes as she caught a glimpse of the trap door in the rear of the flannels. "Jackson, darlin'," Maggie said through her giggles. "You may have to learn some modesty now that we've got another female in the house."

He turned and looked back at his behind. "Why?

They're hitched up and fastened good enough. What's she all fire blushin' about?"

Maggie chuckled, and when he had closed the door behind him she stood to leave as well. "Forgive my boys, Annie. They're daddy didn't care much for modesty either. It's like bangin' my head against a brick wall tryin' to keep them decent at all. Go to sleep, pretty baby. It'll all be right in the mornin'."

∽

Amazingly enough, Annie did fall asleep, and quickly. And slept soundly until morning. The first thing she heard as she drifted away from slumber and into the day was a meadowlark's song carried through the open window on the cool morning breeze. The smell of peaches was sweet and strong on the air, too.

She could hear low-pitched voices coming from the other room and she guessed that the McCall boys and their precious mama had been up and about for some time. She felt happy and safe again. For the first time since...since she couldn't remember.

Quickly she dressed and braided her hair. Taking a deep breath she opened her door. Sunshine radiated through the kitchen windows and she had been right, for the three men and their mother were finishing up breakfast. Annie began to salivate as the aroma of frying bacon and hot maple syrup filled her senses.

"Good mornin', Annie!" Maggie chirped with a broad smile.

Baker smiled broadly at her and she returned the greeting. Annie had already decided that this man's moods were contagious. "Well. Let me just tell you, Miss Annie...that you better be dang glad I ain't the one who found you lyin' out there...'cause I would've just run off with you all to myself. Jackson ain't got the sense given a pig."

"I'm done, Mama. I'll be in the north pasture if you need me," Matt said, rising from the table and kissing his mother's cheek. "Baker can complain all he wants to about chasin' down ol' Root, but seems like I'm the one always gets stuck with repairin' that north fence when he busts it down. You have a good day, Annie...and don't let Mama run you ragged just yet." He tipped his hat with a smile and headed out the back door.

"Hello!" Mary called from the front door.

"Come on in, honey!" Maggie said, wiping her hands on her checkered apron. "I'm glad you're here. Now we can get started as soon as Annie's had her breakfast. Have you eaten, Mary?"

"Oh, yes, ma'am. You know my mama...don't matter if she starves you the rest of the day...we all eat breakfast whether or not we want to," Mary said as Annie noticed her eyes lingering on the back of Jackson's head.

"Me and Baker are gonna break in that new black today, Mama," Jackson mumbled as he wiped his mouth with a white napkin.

"Oh, no! Jackson...surely not yet. He's so wild! I wish you would geld him instead of usin' him for stud. He frightens me." Maggie said. "I hate when you go a breakin' in horses as wild as that one. Bill scares me even now."

"Oh, Mama...you worry too much. You know big brother can break any horse alive. I'd put money on it any day of the week," Baker assured her, looking at his brother who grinned back at him.

"Dang right," Jackson said, slapping Baker's broad shoulder.

"You see, Annie," Maggie began, "my boy Jackson here, thinks there ain't a horse on this green earth that he can't ride. I'll admit...he's bred some mighty fine colts and fillies...made a heap of money doin' it. But you watch him a bit today and tell me if it was your baby out there, how you'd feel. Besides, there's always your daddy to consider, Jackson."

The boys' smiles faded.

"Now, Mama...don't you worry about me. I won't take no unnecessary chances," Jackson assured her.

"It's unnecessary to break him at all, son."

Baker stood and kissed his mother affectionately on the forehead. "Don't you worry, Mama. That's why I go with him. To keep his head on his shoulders, 'stead of smashed in the dirt. Ladies," he said, tipping his hat as he put it on. "Do come out for a visit later after Mama has you sick of peaches." And he left.

Jackson stood up and kissed his Mama as well. "Don't you girls let her sit in here and fret all mornin'. He's not as bad as you think, Mama. Girls," he said with a smile and followed his brother out.

Annie didn't miss the look that passed between Mary and Jackson as he had turned to leave, and for some reason she felt resentful of it.

"I hope they're careful, Mrs. McCall," Mary said, frowning.

Maggie let out a heavy sigh. "Well, darlin's...when you have boys you better strengthen your faith. Now let's do some peaches. You haven't said one word this mornin', Annie. Not that you could get one in around here during breakfast."

"It's far more entertaining to listen to ya'll talking," she said, smiling. "By the way, Mrs. McCall...I'm afraid I don't know whether or not I've ever done any canning."

Mary giggled. "Well, it's easy enough, Annie. Just takes time."

芯

They canned for nearly five hours without a break and Annie found it exhilarating. They talked and Maggie and Mary gossiped. Annie learned a lot just listening to them. The most disturbing to her was Mary's habit of bringing the conversation around to Jackson nearly constantly. She didn't know why it bothered her so. Jackson obviously looked upon Mary with some affection, at least. Whereas he seemed to think Annie a great inconvenience.

"Those boys get so busy. I hate when they don't come in for lunch. Mary, take Annie out there to the corral to call those two in for lunch. I'll go holler for Matthew," Maggie sighed.

Mary gleefully slipped her arm through Annie's and led her out through the door and down to the corrals.

Annie had never seen such a sight, she was sure.

There was Baker sitting atop the fence hollering as he watched his brother. Jackson was astride a magnificent black stallion which was jumping and arching his back furiously, trying to throw the determined looking man off. Mary leaned up against the fence but Annie felt nervous and stood back a few feet.

"Is he gettin' anywhere, Baker?" Mary asked.

"Oh yeah! Look at that! He's nearly got him now!"

"He does?" Annie inquired doubtfully. She couldn't help moving closer to the fence to get a better look.

"Oh yeah!" Baker chuckled, reaching back, grabbing her arm and pulling her flush with the fence. The dust being kicked up made it hard to breathe.

"YeeeHaw!" Baker hollered. "You got him now, brother! He's wearin' down!"

"He is?" Annie asked again. She wondered how in the world Jackson was staying on that horse.

And in the very next moment, he wasn't. She watched in horror as Jackson's seat left the horse's back and landed hard on the ground. Then she stifled a scream as she watched the horse stomp at him as he ran to the fence and jumped it. The horse snorted and shook his head furiously, rearing and stomping savagely.

"You sorry cuss," Jackson muttered, clearing the fence just in time.

"Jackson...your mama wants you boys in for some lunch. But you're covered in dirt!" Mary laughed. "She'll have your hide if you go trackin' in like that."

"Then I won't go trackin' in, Mary. Now give me

a big hug and a kiss, girl," Jackson said, moving to capture Mary in his arms.

"No!" she screamed as she giggled and moved away. "You're filthy!"

Baker chuckled. "It's just good ol' dust, Mary."

"He's filthy!" she laughed.

Jackson grinned slyly at her. He was dusty, Annie admitted. But it was different than being dirty.

"Soil doesn't make a man filthy," she thought out loud. "A man can be as clean and smell as fresh as evening and still be the filthiest creature on this earth." Annie hugged herself tightly as she broke out in goose bumps. Something was making her feel sick to her stomach. Something dreadful.

"Well, thank you, Miss Annie," Jackson said, bowing. "Coming from you...that's a real compliment."

She was suddenly rather vexed. Why was he so mocking? "What do you mean by that?" she demanded and his eyebrows rose in surprise. "What have I done that has caused you to label me as arrogant? Nothing I'm aware of. In fact, I would say you are the more uppity of the two of us! Overly judgmental of people that you know absolutely nothing about! Why did you even bother bringing me here if I'm such an annoyance to you?"

Jackson stood staring with a stunned expression on his face.

"Well," Baker said, grinning. "We know she has a fuse about as short as Mama's at least."

"I'm sorry, Mr. McCall," Annie said, smoothing her

skirt self-consciously. "I'm just overly fatigued, I guess. I must seem terribly ungrateful to you." She put a hand to her head as she felt a sudden headache hit.

"Not at all, Annie. I'm sorry if I made you feel unwelcome," Jackson apologized, grinning almost kindly at her.

"Your mama is gonna think we got lost comin' to get you boys," Mary reminded. "You all right, Annie?" she asked when she noticed the frown on the girl's face.

"I'm fine," she whispered.

"Maybe it's this hot air not agreein' with you," Baker suggested, tipping her head up and searching her face.

"No. No. Actually, I find it much nicer than all that sticky dampness. A body can't even dry off after bathing, there's so much moisture in the air there," she mumbled as she began to feel dizzy. Suddenly she was shaken back to her senses by Jackson's strong hands on her shoulders.

"What do you mean? Where is it damp? Where?" he growled into her face.

"Dang it, Jack. Give her some air." Baker said, removing his brother's grip and scooping Annie up in his arms. And then everything was dark.

Annie regained consciousness almost immediately. "Put me down! Please, Baker!" she demanded, feeling completely aggravated. "I'm fine. It's only a headache." She was not the weak blooded, silly girl they were taking her for. She pushed firmly against Baker's broad chest until he put her down.

"You sure you're all right, Annie?" he asked, sincerely concerned.

She looked up into his handsome face and felt the urge to smooth the frown from his brow. Smiling she said, "I'm fine. I'm sorry to be so much trouble." Mary and Jackson looked at each other and then at her.

"Where is it so damp and all, Annie?" Jackson asked casually.

Annie tossed her head and rolled her eyes. "Louisiana, of course! Where else would I be..." her voice trailed off and the others watched as the color drained from her face.

"Louisiana? Where in Louisiana?" Jackson asked, taking several steps forward until he stood directly in front of her with his eyes burning into hers.

"Just...Louisiana," she choked out.

"Jackson," Baker said, taking his brother firmly by the arm. "That's good, darlin'," he continued. "You're beginnin' to remember. See. Now, let's get in there for lunch before Mama has kittens."

Still holding his elder brother by the arm, Baker pushed Jackson ahead of himself and through the screen door.

"What's the matter with you all?" Maggie asked when she noticed the two brothers glaring at each other as they washed up in the basin.

"Nothin'," Baker answered bluntly.

"Mary? Annie? Now I know you girls will tell me what's goin' on. You weren't hurt tryin' to break that horse were you, Jackson?" she asked.

Mary looked at Annie and then cast her eyes to the floor. "I think I must have come here from Louisiana, Mrs. McCall. In fact, I'm sure that's where I'm from. I think your eldest son is impatient and irritated with me because I can't remember anything else. That's all."

The cloudy memory, as small as it was, was gradually helping Annie's confidence and personality to re-emerge. She felt that maybe she would eventually be able to remember everything. And that no matter what, she could endure it. She had felt like a little lost puppy until now. But that would change. She hoped.

"That's wonderful, honey!" Maggie exclaimed, but Annie thought she sensed a look of regret in the woman's eyes. "Now, you take Jackson with a grain of salt, dear. He's an impatient boy. And, Jackson McCall, you find some manners and compassion in that hard heart of yours."

"Oh, he's not so hard-hearted, Mrs. McCall. It's an act, I think," Mary said, coyly smiling at Jackson.

Annie didn't miss the look in Mary's eyes as she watched Jackson sit down at the table next to her.

"Got that mean thing broke yet, Jackson?" Matthew asked as he came through the back door and began to clean up at the basin.

"Give me another hour or two, little brother. He ain't as tough as he lets on," Jackson answered, smiling.

"Most people ain't either," Baker said, winking at Annie and motioning subtly at his elder brother.

As Matthew sat down Annie noticed how his eyes lingered on Mary for a moment then darted around nervously to see if anyone had noticed. Mary's gaze never left Jackson, though he seemed oblivious to the fact. Annie felt a little stitch form in the pit of her stomach. Obviously Matthew had feelings for Mary, and obviously Mary had eyes only for Jackson who didn't seem to be aware of it.

"Why don't you tell us about Louisiana, Annie," Jackson suggested after they had begun their meal.

"Good gravy, Jackson! Leave the girl alone," Maggie exclaimed.

"It's okay, Mrs. McCall," Annie said, sensing the tone of almost 'I don't believe you' in Jackson's voice. "I don't remember much, Mr. McCall. It's a feeling almost more than a vision. Moist, heavy air. Rain. The smell of a million different green things and a million different bug noises in the breeze. Magnolias come to mind. And grand old, black oaks." Suddenly a shiver went through her. The dream she had had the night before returned and for a moment she was silent as she tried to remember more about it.

"What makes you sure that it's Louisiana you're rememberin'?" Baker asked.

"I'm uncertain," she answered, hugging herself to dispel the goose bumps that had sprung up all over her.

"I take it that our Annie here is from Louisiana," Matthew stated. "Not that anybody bothers tellin' me anything nohow."

"I think she's the very picture of what I've heard a Creole girl should look like," Mary added. "They've all got dark hair, milky skin, and are as beautiful as princesses," she added in a dreamy voice.

"Well, then I'm surely not a Creole girl," Annie added in complete sincerity. When she looked up from her plate, everyone at the table was staring at her with odd expressions on their faces.

"At least she's humble about it," Jackson said, chuckling and returning his attention to his food.

Matthew stood to leave. "Thank you, Mama. I feel a whole lot better. Ready to run down ol' Root now. He got out while I was repairin' that fence. Wanna help me, Baker? You seem to have a regular talent in catchin' that bull."

Baker shook his head vigorously. "You kiddin'? What would ol' Jackson do without me out there to make sure he don't get hurt. Naw. You better take care of ol' Root yourself, Matt."

"I'll come with you, Matthew," Annie volunteered, standing up and folding her napkin neatly.

"I don't know, Annie..." Matthew began to protest.

"I'll be fine. I just can't imagine a ring in a cow's nose. I've got to see that for myself."

"Bull, Annie. Ol' Root is a bull," Maggie chuckled.

Matthew glanced at Mary who was still staring dumbly at Jackson, who was still cleaning his plate.

"Okay, Annie. You a fast runner?" he asked, and they left laughing.

CHAPTER FOUR

"What's the matter, Matthew?" Annie asked, surprising the man.

"What do you mean?" He stopped walking and looked curiously down at her.

"You like Mary, don't you, Matthew?" she asked.

He looked away rolling his eyes as if he thought it a silly question. "You're loco, Annie. Mary's been in love with Jackson since she was six years old. She asked him to marry her when she was thirteen. Why would I be interested in her?"

"Because she's pretty, and sweet. You're nearly completely silent whenever she's around, you know."

He began walking again. "Where has that bull gone off to?"

Annie was beginning to feel that maybe her feet weren't used to walking through pastures and climbing fences. But as far as her encouraging Matthew where Mary was concerned, she was undaunted. "Maybe if you weren't so silent...more yourself when she was around...she'd notice you," she went on.

Matthew laughed and stopped, looking down at

her. "You're a persistent little gal, you know that? You don't even know me, Annie. How are you so sure who I like and what I should do about it?" His smile was like sunshine.

"It's a gift I have, Matthew. Truly it is. You just need to catch her attention."

He took her hand in his own and patted it with the other. "I've seen other men try to take women's attention away from my big brother, Annie. It don't happen. They're always second choice once the female realizes that Jackson won't ever be interested. I don't want to be second choice, Annie. I'll wait for a girl who sees me first."

"She's just infatuated, Matthew. He's quite rough, mysterious...she'll get over him, I'm sure," Annie encouraged.

"You are a sweet thing, Annie. But I'm a lost cause. Hey! There he is! Come on!" And he took off toward an enormous bull standing some one hundred feet away.

Annie hiked up her dress and petticoats and took out after him. She stopped when they got close and the bull lowered his head and snorted. He looked mean and Annie didn't like the ominous look of his horns.

"Matthew?" she whispered. She could clearly see the shiny copper ring that pierced the animal's nose.

"Oh, he's full of beans and other stuff, Annie. Don't worry."

But when the bull started on a headlong run straight for her, she turned and began to run.

"Jump the fence, Annie!" she heard Matthew holler,

and she obeyed, rather ungracefully, when she reached it.

The bull charged headlong into the fence and she let out a startled scream as she turned to see him ramming it over and over again with his massive head. Matthew reached him finally and jerked hard on the ring protruding from Root's nose. The bull turned his head and Matthew began to lead him back to the pasture.

He looked back at Annie, who was still panting from her sprint, and called, "He'll get to know you, Annie. You run on back to the house and tell ol' Baker he ain't the only one 'round here that sticks in ol' Root's craw!"

Matthew's laughter was contagious and Annie giggled to herself. What a sight she must have been!

When she entered the house, it was to hear Maggie's concerned voice scolding Jackson.

"I knew it! I knew it! That horse is mean, Jackson! Look at this! He could've really hurt you!"

"Mama, I've been nipped before...it ain't no big..." Jackson started.

"Nipped? Nipped? Jackson, it's beyond me, son, how this is considered a nip!"

Jackson was standing in the kitchen taking off his shirt and Maggie was frantically wetting a towel at the basin.

"Mary, fetch some water and get it boilin'! Oh, Annie! Thank goodness! Get that boy to sit down!"

Annie looked at her dumbfounded. What did she mean? Was she to command him to 'sit'?

"Just look at that! Will you look at that?" Maggie exclaimed.

"Mama, go out and gather the eggs or somethin'. Please. Baker and Annie can take care of this," Jackson said calmly.

Annie stood still, not quite knowing what to do.

"Jackson. Quit ordering me around. I'm your mama!" Maggie wailed frantically.

"I've helped with horse bites before, Mrs. McCall. I can do it. You go out for some air," Annie said, understanding the situation at once.

"I just don't handle it well when my babies get hurt, Annie. I don't handle it well at all," she said, wiping the perspiration from her brow.

Mary returned and handed the water to Annie.

"Mary, take Mama out for a walk, will you?" Baker said, winking at Annie and handing his mother to Mary.

"Come on, Mrs. McCall. Let's get you some air," Mary suggested, leading the woman out the door.

"Those boys!" Maggie sighed heavily as she left. "They keep my stomach in knots! I'll probably end up with twenty-five grandsons and not one granddaughter in the litter."

"It is a pretty bad one, Jack," Baker said, examining the bite mark on Jackson's shoulder.

"Well, it feels pretty bad. That ol' cuss. Nipped me when I had my back turned. I've gotta break him now, Baker. I can't let him get away with it."

"You wanna clean this out, Annie. I ain't too

thorough at cleanin' wounds," Baker said, wrinkling up his nose.

Annie walked over to inspect the wound herself with great reluctance.

"Neked men make her nervous," Jackson whispered to Baker and they both smiled broadly.

"Perhaps," Annie agreed. "But unclad adolescent boys do not concern me in the least."

Baker snickered. "She's gettin' wise to you, Jack," he mumbled to his brother.

The wound was more severe than Annie had first thought. "Do you receive these kinds of injuries on a regular basis?" she asked.

"Yep. Impressive. Ain't it?" he asked, though he grimaced as she pressed on it.

"Where I come from we call it, 'stupidity,'" she stated.

Baker and Jackson raised their eyebrows at each other.

"Well, well, well! Miss High and Mighty, I'm sure that where you come from the boys all smell like girls and ride sidesaddle, too," Jackson chuckled. "You come sit here on my lap and I'll show you what a real, hard workin' man feels like." And he pulled her to sit down on his lap.

She was caught off guard and automatically clutched at his arms for support. He grinned slyly at her and she felt like slapping him. He was either flirting or rude every minute of the day! No in between it seemed.

She intentionally squeezed his wounded shoulder as she righted herself.

"Where I come from, Mister McCall...men like you are welcomed only in brothels and drinking establishments," she informed him as she began to dress the wound.

"I think that it weren't no rag doll you brung home, big brother," Baker chuckled.

Jackson never quit smiling at her the entire time she was dressing the wound, and it made her very self-conscious, though she did an excellent job of hiding it.

Mary returned with Maggie who immediately began smoothing her son's hair and clinging to him. "I wish you wouldn't break so many, son. You know it unnerves me," she pleaded quietly.

"I'm a big boy, Mama. And horses need to be broke if we're gonna sell 'em." Then he stood up, took Annie's hand and pressed it against his bare chest. "And thank you, Miss Annie. You did an excellent job of dressin' this bite." He smiled as she began to blush and tried to pull her hand away from his hot skin.

"I take it that you never had brothers, Annie," Mary said, smiling as Annie was able to detach her hand at last.

"You're rotten to the core, Jackson. And put a shirt back on. For cryin' in the bucket, son! Have some manners." Maggie scolded, although her smile was as broad as everyone else's, except Annie's.

"Come on, Baker. Let's break that ol' sucker." Jackson said, putting his blood stained shirt back on

42

and heading out the door.

"You're going to let him go out there again?" Annie questioned Maggie in disbelief.

"I don't want to, honey...but that horse has gotta learn who's boss," the older woman replied.

CHAPTER FIVE

After two weeks, Annie was feeling quite comfortable at the McCall ranch. She hadn't remembered anything else. Just bits and pieces of Louisiana life. She had fallen into a routine of daily chores and loved them. Milking a cow every morning, gathering eggs, churning butter, making soap, mending, helping to bring in the herds in the evening, etc. She loved the life the McCalls led and secretly hoped it would go on forever.

The boys were wonderful to her. Except for Jackson, who seemed to like her one minute and be irritated with her the next. Matthew still pined for Mary from afar and she was still unaware of it. Mary spent a lot of time at the ranch and Annie found herself annoyed each time she would see the girl smiling cutely at Jackson and tugging at his shirt sleeve to get his attention.

One morning Annie went out as usual to milk Flossy. She went to the corner of the barn for a stool and heard voices. Jackson and Mary were coming into the barn and she was certain that Mary sounded upset. For some reason, Annie quickly hid in an empty stall instead of revealing that she was there.

"Jackson, don't you care for me at all?" Mary sniffled in a pain stricken voice.

"Of course I do, Mary. But not like you're wantin' me to. We've had this conversation before," Jackson sounded angry.

"But, Jackson…I've grown up now. I'm old enough for you. I'd do anything for you!"

Annie found a knothole in one of the boards of the stall and peered through it.

Jackson spun around and took Mary by the shoulders. "Listen to me, Mary. I don't want to upset you, and I never, ever wanted to hurt you. But it's just not gonna be, darlin'. I always thought you'd outgrow your crush..."

"It's not a crush anymore, Jackson!" Mary interrupted furiously. "Just let me prove it to you, Jackson…I'm old enough to be everythin' you need...and want."

Annie's eyes widened as she watched Mary lock her fingers behind the man's neck. Her expression then changed from hurt and frustration to something quite different.

"Mary, I'm serious. I'm not for you. You're a sweet, beautiful young lady. You deserve much better than a smelly ol' cowboy like me," Jackson said quietly, trying to remove her arms from about his neck.

"You are for me, Jackson. You've always been for me. I grew up...just for you." The girl raised herself to kiss him but he turned his head from her and she only succeeded in kissing his handsome, unshaven face.

Jackson forcefully removed her arms from around

him and held them to her sides. "Enough, Mary. It won't ever be. You need to go on with your life."

"You are my life, Jackson!" she pleaded.

"No, Mary. I'm not what you need and, I'm sorry, but you're not what I need. And…and you're not what I want."

Annie suddenly felt sorry for the girl. The look on Mary's face was that of utter and complete heartbreak.

"I'm sorry, Mary. If I ever led you to believe anythin' could happen between us…I'm sorry," Jackson soothed as the tears began to roll down Mary's cheeks.

"You've nothin' to be sorry for, Jackson. It was me. I know that. You never led me on in any way. I'll leave you alone. I'm the one who's sorry."

She turned to flee, but Jackson caught her arm and pulled her to him holding her in a sweet embrace. "You've always been special to me, darlin'. I don't want you hatin' me or stayin' away because of me. Everyone loves you here. You're like one of the family. Don't stay angry with me. I'm just a nasty old bear…not much good for anythin' but breakin' horses and fightin' with my fists." Then he cupped her face in his hands and kissed her lightly on the mouth. "Now then…we've had our kiss. Someday, when you're married with ten babies runnin' around in the barn yard, you'll look over at your handsome devil of a husband and think…'That ol' Jackson McCall…he weren't hardly worth all the fuss.'"

Mary smiled up at him through her tears. "You're wrong, Jackson. You're wrong."

He grinned at her as he gently pushed her away

from him after a final hug. "Nope. I'm right. You'll see, darlin'. You'll see."

Mary smiled at him once more, turned and left, wiping her tears on her apron. "I better get back and help your mama with those berries."

Annie wiped a tear from her own cheek and whispered to herself, "How sad." Then terror struck as she saw Jackson turn his attention to her hiding place.

Looking as fierce as ol' Root, he reached over the wall, grabbing the back of her dress and pulling her up to face him.

"I understand why you hid. You didn't have much time to do anythin' else. But if you care anythin' at all for our little Mary...you'll forget everythin' you heard. She's a sweet girl and I won't have her embarrassed."

Annie grabbed his arm that held her dress and dug her fingernails in deep. "Let me go!" she growled at him. "I'd never do anything to hurt Mary! Even you should know that."

Jackson released Annie and his expression was now that of discouragement. "I hate situations like that. I never handle them right," he mumbled, picking up a pitchfork and starting to clean the stall. It really bothered him. Annie knew that it did. It dripped from every part of him.

"You handled it wonderfully. Many men would've laughed at her. Or worse, taken advantage of the situation."

"I suppose," he mumbled.

He was so incredibly handsome! Annie understood

how a girl could be in love with him from the day she was born.

"You better get to milkin' that cow before she busts," he said, smiling at her.

She blushed when she realized that she had been staring at him.

"I have to say, Miss Annie. I misjudged you. You turned out to be a right good worker. Even if you ain't got calloused hands," Jackson chuckled when she had finished milking Flossy.

Annie smiled as she lifted the bucket full of milk and began to leave. "Thank you. I know how it pains you to admit you were wrong."

Annie left the barn and began to walk toward the house, but she stopped in her tracks when she saw them. A group of wild looking Indians was approaching on horseback. When they saw her they stopped and the one who appeared to be their leader dismounted his horse and moved toward her.

"Jackson?" her voice squeaked out. She couldn't yell. She was too frightened. So she slowly set the bucket down and began walking backwards toward the barn. They looked so menacing!

As she walked backwards, the Indian still walked toward her. When she felt a pair of hands on her shoulders she gasped and spun around. Relief flooded her as Jackson pulled her into his arms and against his strong, protective body.

"What do you want here, Black Wolf?" he asked angrily. There was no response. "We've nothing to trade today. I want you to go," Jackson growled.

"The woman. She is very good to look at," came the rough reply of the Indian.

A chill of horror traveled down Annie's spine and she wrapped her arms tightly around Jackson's waist.

Jackson said nothing at first, then began stroking her hair, as he said, "She's mine. Don't look at her."

The Indian chuckled. "I will trade many horses for her, Captain. I know that you want horses. I want the woman. We have seen her in the field many times. I will take her and you can have horses. Or I will take her and your life can bleed from you." Annie clenched her arms tightly around Jackson's waist, but he broke the embrace and pushed her aside. Without Jackson's support, Annie's knees weakened and she found herself trembling and sitting on the ground at his feet.

"Don't threaten me, Black Wolf. You know I have no fear of you. And you also know that I can kill you easily. Now leave. Or *your* life will end. You're never to come here again. Never come near this land...or you will die."

Annie looked up at Black Wolf. His expression was one of barely controlled anger as he looked at her. His chest rose and fell with his angry breathing.

"She is your woman?" Black Wolf asked.

"Yes," Jackson replied. "Never dare to even look at her again, Black Wolf."

The Indian took a deep breath and forced a smile. "Of course, Captain. Black Wolf understands." And he offered a hand to Jackson.

Jackson shook his hand briefly, but never smiled. He stood like a granite boulder watching them ride away. Then turned to look at Annie. She still sat on the ground next to him shaking with fright.

"I saw them out near the north pasture two days ago. I had no idea what he was lookin' for...until now," Jackson mumbled.

Annie felt an odd guilt rush through her. She had put this wonderful family in danger. She wanted to find a hole and crawl into it.

"He called you 'Captain,'" she whispered. Jackson just shrugged his shoulders and offered her a hand to help her up.

"Let me tell Mama, Annie. It makes her mighty nervous whenever they show up."

She put her hand in his and quickly removed it once she had stood. "They're very shocking...aren't they? I mean...the first time you ever see them." She tried to speak calmly, but her voice still quivered, revealing the state of her nerves.

"They're renegades. A mess of different tribes... Apache, Crow...all pretty mean. But they're alone out here so they stay pretty much in hand." Then he took her by the shoulders and glared into her face. "Never show your fear! They take it as a sign of weakness. Talk confidently...trade with them. But never give them anything."

"You think they'll come back...don't you?"

He shrugged again. "You might wanna get that milk

into Mama before the flies get to it." And he turned and walked back into the barn.

∽

"Well! I was wonderin' where you had gone off to, honey," Maggie chirped as Annie entered the kitchen. "What's wrong?" she asked immediately as she continued to look at the girl. "You're as white as a sheet."

Annie tried to smile. Why shouldn't she be pale. In the last ten minutes she had witnessed Jackson breaking Mary's heart and nearly been abducted by renegade Indians. "I'm fine, Mrs. McCall. Too much sun maybe."

Maggie wiped her hands on her apron and felt Annie's forehead. "Too much sun, my foot! Now you tell me what has you lookin' so peaked."

"Ol' Black Wolf just paid us a visit, Mama. I suspect little Miss Annie was a little...unnerved," Jackson said, striding through the back door with a broad smile.

"Black Wolf!" Maggie gasped, all color draining from her face as well. "What did he want, son?" she asked.

Jackson cleared his throat, grabbed a fresh peach from the basket on the table, and began peeling it with a pocketknife. "Annie," he answered, nodding toward the girl.

Maggie's mouth dropped open and she looked from Jackson to Annie and back again. "Annie?" she whispered. "Tell me you're teasing me, Jack!"

"Nope. He wanted little miss porcelain complexion, here."

Annie felt tears of exasperation brimming in her eyes. He could be so insensitive!

"What did you tell him?" Maggie asked, pulling a chair from the table and sitting down.

Jackson's smile faded. "Don't worry, Mama. He won't be back."

Maggie clutched his hand firmly in hers and spoke gravely, "Jackson...how can you be sure?"

Jackson looked up at Annie, then back to his mother. "I didn't have to say anythin'. He got a closer look at her and changed his mind."

For a moment Maggie's expression was still that of worry, but it slowly changed to a smile.

Annie, however, found nothing soothing or humorous in his remark and as the tears of frustration began to escape her eyes she slammed the bucket of milk down on the table and fled out the back door.

As she angrily walked away, she began to realize that she felt more hurt than vexed. She didn't like the fact that she was a burden to Jackson McCall--an irritating inconvenience. The two times she had been in his embrace, when he held her as they rode home after his finding her and as he spoke to the Indian only a few minutes before, she had felt safe, protected and as if she wanted to stay only there forever. But he obviously saw her as nothing more than an ignorant girl who was a burden to the family.

"Wait a minute, jumpin' bean," Jackson chuckled as

he caught her elbow and spun her around to face him. "You know I was only kiddin'! Mama gets so upset when Black Wolf is roamin' around. I had to calm her down."

Annie yanked her arm from his grasp and began walking away. "Fine. Now let me go for a walk. It has been a very fatiguing day." She wiped the tears from her cheeks and continued marching off.

Again he grabbed her arm to stay her. "Looky here, Miss Annie," he said, glaring at her. "I don't go chasin' after emotionally high strung women as a rule...so you hear me out."

"I am not emotionally high strung, Mr. McCall! I've just been nearly abducted by wild Renegades and drug off to who knows what...and you're making light of it." He took a deep breath as Annie continued her venting. "I am sorry that you had to be the one to bear the burden of finding me out in the wilderness. But until I remember some shred of my life before you were forced to rescue me...I'll have to stay here and be the proverbial thorn in your side. Forgive me! Will you... and quit bringing the fact of my complete dependency to my attention every living minute of the day!"

Jackson's eyebrows raised in slight surprise at her outburst.

"Okay," he said. Annie took a deep breath and smoothed her skirt. "Maybe you didn't run away, Annie. Maybe you talked somebody crazy and they dumped you out there," he muttered with a grin.

She moved to slap his face but he caught her hand

and twisted her arm behind her pulling her body flush with his. The ache in her chest of hurt at his words started again.

"Why do you hate me so much," she whispered as more tears escaped her eyes.

She looked up into his face, which was solemn again. His eyes left hers and seemed to rest on her mouth for just an instant. She glanced away from him when she realized that she had been studying his mouth as well.

"I don't hate you. I just like to tease, that's all," he whispered. Then he abruptly let her go. "If you ever see Black Wolf again, Annie...you get on back to the house at once and tell one of us boys. Do you understand?" He was so commanding, she felt like saluting with a strong 'Yes, sir!' But she only nodded.

"Now, go for your walk and think hateful things about me." He smiled, tipping his hat and began walking away.

He paused for a moment and said, "You won't let anyone know what you heard in the barn before, will you?"

"Of course not! I like Mary and I'd never want to embarrass her," she replied.

"Did I...did I handle that all right, do you think?" he asked, adjusting his hat.

Annie was astonished. He actually seemed unsure about something. "Yes, of course," she muttered and watched him leave.

CHAPTER SIX

That night at dinner the inevitable subject of Black Wolf came up.

"What did he want, Jackson?" Baker asked.

"Annie," Jackson replied, glancing at Annie and then his mama.

"Annie?" Matthew repeated.

"Well, I think that's mighty understandable," Baker said, smiling at Annie and adding a wink.

"It's terrifying!" Maggie reminded.

"Well, what did you tell him, Jack?" Matthew asked.

Jackson spread some butter on a biscuit before answering nonchalantly. "I told him that he couldn't have her 'cause she was mine."

Baker and Matthew raised their eyebrows at each other. Matthew let out an amazed whistle.

"Now my question is this," Baker began smiling, "did you tell him that to avoid a situation like the Smithes had...or were you thinkin' 'finders keepers'?" Baker winked at Annie again.

But Annie noticed that Maggie had dropped her fork.

"The Smithes?" Maggie asked as an ill looking paleness washed over her.

"Good job, Baker," Matthew mumbled, hitting his brother hard in the ribs with an elbow.

"Now, Mama, don't get all upset," Jackson began.

"The Smithe girl! They took her and...well...Jackson, are you sure Annie's safe now?"

"What happened to the Smithe girl?" Annie asked as she felt the hair on the back of her neck stand on end.

"Mama, Bill Smithe didn't know a thing about dealin' with Them renegades. These renegades...they aren't like the friendlier tribes. You gotta play tough. I told Black Wolf that she was mine. He knows not to buck any of us boys. He thinks she's mine...Bill Smithe told them other renegades that his daughter, Lilly, didn't belong to nobody. Black Wolf won't cross me, Mama. You know it."

Maggie threw her napkin down. "I don't know it, son! This frightens me!" Then she turned to Annie. "Lilly Smithe was taken by renegades. They did unspeakable things to her, Annie! Then they took her back to her daddy and murdered her right in front of him."

Annie looked at Jackson who returned to eating his meal.

"Um...Mama," Matthew ventured. "I don't know if you wanna get too all detailed about that story just now." Then he turned to Annie. "Black Wolf is scared of Jackson, Annie. He's scared of all us boys. You ain't got nothin' to worry about."

"That's right, darlin'" Baker said, reaching across the table and taking her hand. "You got three knights in shinin' armor here to protect you. You're safer here than you've ever been in your life, I'll bet."

His smile was so contagious, but Annie startled when Jackson reached out and slapped Baker's hand, causing him to release hers.

"She's mine remember, little brother?" he said chuckling.

"It's not funny!" Maggie cried out. Everyone looked at her. She wore a terrified expression. "Are you sure, Jackson?" she asked in a whisper.

He smiled warmly at his mother. "I'm sure, Mama. And if he did come back, I can whip him. So, don't worry."

"He's a beast, Jackson! He'd carve you up like that girl!" she sobbed.

Jackson got up from the table. He walked over and crouched down beside his mother. "No one's gonna carve me up, Mama. I'm too mean," he whispered lowly.

The woman took the man's face in her hands, kissed his forehead and smiled. "You're my pretty baby, son. I just worry," she whispered.

"Nothin' to worry about, Mama," he assured her.

Annie felt panic rising in her bosom. She had to get away! She was putting this precious group of people in obvious danger. But what could she do?

"Excuse me," she said, smiling and pushing her chair back.

"You all right, darlin'?" Maggie asked.

"Fine. Fine," Annie said smiling. "Just need a little air." And she walked out the back door and toward the barn.

Her mind began racing. How could she get away? Where could she go? These people who had taken her in and cared for her were in danger! She could go to the sheriff. Maybe someone was looking for her. She could have Mary go into town toorrow and check. She didn't have any money for a train ticket to anywhere. No horse or supplies to ride away with.

"Stop it right now, Annie," Jackson spoke from behind her. She spun around, startled.

"What?" she asked.

"I know what you're thinkin'. Stop it. You're not goin' anywhere."

"But I've put you all in terrible danger! If I leave..."

"If you leave, it'll break my mama's heart. And we don't like to have our mama upset. I'll tie you up in your room if you don't stop thinkin' this way. Understand?"

She looked up at him with desperation in her eyes. "You could help me. Just give me the means to buy a ticket east. I can go somewhere and get a job! I'm a burden to you all here."

"Oh quit playin' martyr, Annie. You're no burden. Mama needs to have you here. You're good company for her. And besides...it gives us boys somethin' to look at besides the hitchin' post." He flashed a brilliant smile at her.

But there was more that she couldn't tell him. She

was following in Mary's footsteps. She felt nervous whenever he was near her. Her bosom ached whenever he almost touched her in some way. She dreamt of him...thought of him almost constantly during the idle and working hours of the day. She found herself watching his mouth when he talked and wondering what his kiss would feel like.

"Hey!" Baker's voice boomed as he approached. "What are you two doin' out here? Are you tryin' to start sparkin' with my girl, Jack?" He laughed and put a comforting arm around Annie's shoulders. "We all know what you're thinkin', sweet pea. And Jackson may mean well, but he's got as much charm as ol' Root. You ain't puttin' us out, or in danger or inconveniencin' us in any way...other than I gotta listen to Jackson talkin' in his sleep every night now. But we couldn't very well let him sleep in his old room with you...now could we?"

"I don't know," Jackson said grinning. "I never thought of that before. I'm sure Annie don't snore as loud as you."

Annie reached up and patted Baker warmly on one rough, unshaven cheek. "You always make me feel better, Baker. Thank you."

He smiled and pointed to his other cheek. "Well, then I at least deserve a little peck...don't you think?"

She giggled and smiled as she stood on tiptoe and planted an affectionate kiss on his cheek.

"Hey!" Matthew called from the door. "What's goin' on? After all, Annie, ain't I the one that shares secrets with you?" he said, pointing to his own cheek and bending down.

Annie giggled again and placed a quick kiss on his cheek as well.

"Well, I'm the one that fought off them renegades today, ain't I?" Jackson added, pointing to his cheek.

Annie's smile faded and she felt butterflies take flight in her stomach.

"He don't bite, Annie. Really," Baker chuckled.

She stood before him and just as her lips would've brushed his cheek, he turned his head, causing her to kiss him directly on the mouth instead.

"Slap him, Annie!" Matthew chuckled. "He's slick as ice."

Jackson smiled slyly down at her and she blushed.

"Red is definitely your color, darlin'," he whispered, grinning triumphantly before heading for the barn.

"He's still a kid when it comes to some things, Annie. Now come on in. Mama's still upset," Baker laughed as he put a comforting arm around her shoulders.

After convincing Maggie that she shouldn't worry, Annie went to her room to prepare for bed. She was still shaken by Jackson's boyish gesture at stealing a kiss. He was a puzzle. Serious one minute, boyish and playful the next. And even though it had lasted only a split second, she could still feel his lips brushing hers and smell the familiar scent of leather and hay that was him.

CHAPTER SEVEN

Several days passed before Mary visited again. When she did, she looked solemn and was quiet. Maggie sent a questioning look at Annie more than once and Annie played ignorant to knowing what was wrong with the girl.

At lunch when the boys came in, Annie watched Mary closely. She never once looked at Jackson. She hardly joined in the conversation.

"You feelin' okay, Mary?" Matthew asked.

"Fine. Just quiet today, I guess," she answered, forcing a smile.

"How's your mama, Mary?" Jackson asked, smiling at her warmly.

She glanced at him only briefly before answering, "She's right as rain. We're workin' on our dresses for the Harvest Dance already. Sewin' tires her eyes more now than it used to."

"Harvest Dance?" Annie asked.

Mary's eyes lit up. "Oh! It's just the best thing all year, except for the Christmas Dance, of course! Punkins with faces cut in 'em! Apple Cider! Punkin pie! Waltzin'! Mr. Daniels plays his fiddle and he's wonderful. You'll love it, Annie! I can help you with your dress. Maybe you could do my hair all fancy up for me. I can never do it myself."

Annie smiled. With her simple question she had managed to break the bleakness of the girl's mood.

"Are you gonna go this year, Mrs. McCall?" Mary asked.

Maggie looked skeptical.

"Oh come on, Mama. It'll be so fun if you go with us this year. I mean...someone will have to go with us to chaperon Annie here. It wouldn't look good at all to have us three boys goin' alone with her," Matthew said between food bites.

"Oh...I don't know," Maggie whined.

"Oh, come on, Mrs. McCall. I need someone to keep me company while Annie's dancin' all night long. I'm sure she'll be the prettiest girl there," Mary said, patting Annie's hand.

"Well, I don't think either one of you will be wallflowers, girls. I know several young boys that have their eyes on our own Miss Mary," Jackson remarked before standing up to leave.

Mary smiled at him finally and he winked at her.

"You wanna go for a walk with me, Annie?" Mary asked unexpectedly.

"Of course. Goodness knows I need some exercise. Mrs. McCall, your cooking has turned me into a complete piglet!"

"Sow," Jackson corrected her. "Fully grown female pigs are sows."

"Thank you for enlightening me, Mr. McCall," Annie sneered. "I suppose that would be comparable to referring to a colt's hindquarters instead of a fully matured horse's behind."

"She's gettin' good, Jackson," Matthew mumbled.

Jackson tipped his head in agreement.

The girls linked arms, exited through the back door and headed toward the pasture.

"I guess you've noticed that I'm not quite myself lately, Annie," Mary began and took a deep breath to help hold in tears. Annie knew it was time to listen.

"I spoke to Jackson the other day. You see...I've been so terribly in love with him for as long as I can remember...and, I was tired of waitin' to see if he felt anything for me. I just need to talk to someone about this, Annie. I told him how I felt the other day...out in the barn. I was so sure that he felt somethin' for me. But...as it turns out...he doesn't." She wiped the tears from her cheeks. "I just love him so much, Annie. I feel like I'm just gonna shrivel up and die inside."

"I do understand, Mary," Annie said, smiling at her. "More than you can imagine."

"There'll never be anyone else for me, Annie. Never."

Annie put a comforting arm around her friend's shoulders. "I know you think there won't be, Mary. But there will. There might be somebody close, right this moment, that'll treasure you and love you more than you can fathom. And I think you'll find that he's more suited to you...and you'll love him more than you ever did Jackson."

Mary looked up at Annie and smiled. "Nice speech." They both chuckled and hugged.

Just then the back door slammed and the girls turned to see Matthew walking toward the barn.

"Matthew is so sweet," Annie remarked. "He's got a special way of knowing how people feel. He's very understanding and compassionate."

Mary looked at Annie and smiled knowingly. "You wouldn't be trying to steer me toward my old lover's brother, would you Annie?" she asked.

Annie shook her head innocently. "He's very handsome, too. Don't you think?" Annie added.

They giggled. "Well, Miss Annie," Mary started. "I've got an awful handsome older brother myself who is very interested in meetin' you. Collin is a dream and...what's the matter, Annie? Annie!"

Annie put her hands to her head. The pain was excruciating! Everything was going dark and the name 'Collin' kept echoing through her mind.

"Help me!" she whispered just before she fainted.

CHAPTER EIGHT

She could hear voices. They sounded far away at first. Then closer.

"Is she all right?"

"Yeah. Annie. Wake up."

"We were just talkin' and she grabbed her forehead and fainted. No warnin' that it was comin' on at all."

"Annie?" It was Jackson's voice. "Annie? Wake up now."

"Malaina," she whispered as she began to regain consciousness. "My name is Malaina." She opened her eyes to see Jackson searching her face.

"Malaina?" he repeated. She watched his mouth as he repeated her name. "Malaina. Can you hear me?" he asked.

"I can hear you."

"Do you know who I am?" he commanded.

"You're Jackson McCall. Do you think I'm ignorant?"

Malaina heard chuckling and Jackson smiled. "You know darn well I think you're ignorant. She'll be all right, Mama. Looks like the memory is comin' back, too. Malaina. At least we can go back to namin' the stock 'Annie' now."

Maggie leaned over and smiled at her as she smoothed her hair back. "Malaina. That's a beautiful name. It suits you much better. You had me worried, sweetheart! As if these three boys don't keep my insides stirred up enough as it is."

"I'm sorry," Malaina whispered.

"Anything else? Do you remember your last name?" Jackson asked.

Malaina's head ached brutally. "No. But there's someone evil...a man. I don't know why...but I know he's evil. Collin something. That's all I can remember."

"We were talkin' about my brother, Collin. It musta triggered a memory for her, Mrs. McCall," Mary said.

"We'll go and let you rest, honey," Maggie said with a smile.

"Oh, no! No. I'm fine. Really. I need to get busy if Mary's gonna teach me how to sew a new dress for this Harvest Dance," Malaina said frantically. She didn't want to be left alone.

"Okay, sweet pea. Why don't you and Mary have Matthew drive you into town? The general store should have some cloth that'll do for a dress."

Malaina paused as realization hit her. "On second thought, Mrs. McCall...maybe I better just wear one of the dresses you've already given me."

"Nonsense, child! You'll be needin' some clothes of your own. We might as well start with a dress for the dance," the woman exclaimed.

"But...I don't..." Malaina stammered as she looked up into Jackson's scowling face.

"For cryin' out loud, Mama," he growled. "She's flat broke. Ain't that what you're tryin' to say, girl?"

Maggie broke into laughter. "Is that what you're worried about, sweetie? Well, I'll be. You're part of the family now! Money we have is yours. too."

But Malaina shook her head. "Oh, no, Mrs. McCall. I'm a big enough burden as it is. I can't possibly expect you to..."

Jackson heaved an exasperated sigh. "You know, Miss Malaina...you're sickenin'ly sweet." Then he reached into the pocket of his well-worn pants, pulled out a wad of paper money, turned Malaina's hand palm up and put the money in it. "Now, go to town, buy cloth and make yourself a new dress. We can't have you lookin' like a ragamuffin at that dance. We got our own reputations to protect." After rolling his eyes to show his irritation with the situation, he put his hat on and left.

Malaina sat stunned for a moment and then looked up at Maggie and Mary. Mary's mouth was still gaping open in surprise, but Maggie was smiling maternally, as usual.

"I can't possibly!" Malaina exclaimed at last.

Maggie laughed. "Of course you can, dear. Where do you think I would've gotten the money anyway?"

"Oh, but Mrs. McCall...a lady just doesn't accept money from a gentleman," Malaina began to explain.

"You're out west now, dear...and this is family. We all work together to keep this ranch goin' and we all get paid for it in one way or another. Now let me get

Matthew." And she left Malaina staring at the wad of money in her hand.

"Jimineeee!" Mary squealed. "What I wouldn't give to trade places with you!"

Malaina counted out the money. "It's far too much, I'm sure. I guess I'll just use what I need and then return the rest. But Mary...taking money from a man! It's so improper!"

Mary giggled. "She's right, you know, Malaina. You're gonna have to change your way of thinkin' now. You do chores around here same as anyone else, don't you? Just think of it as your wages. That's all."

Malaina frowned. "I guess so. Well, let's go then. I haven't been anywhere besides church yet, and you can't see the town from there."

❧

Half an hour later they set out for town. Baker decided to go with them, too. Malaina had managed to get Mary to sit up front in the buggy with Matthew and she sat behind them with Baker.

When Matthew and Mary started their own conversation finally, Baker winked at Malaina and whispered, "I know what you're up to. Don't think I don't."

Malaina giggled. "Now all I have to do is to find a suitable young lady for you, Baker." His smile faded and as he looked away she felt she had said something very wrong.

"Not just yet, darlin'," he muttered. He was quiet for a few more moments then looked at her with an apologetic smile. "I ain't quite ready again. And when I am...well, I got you right here, now don't I?"

But she didn't laugh at his flirt. "What do you mean...'again'?" she asked.

He looked away for a moment. "Well, I guess you might as well hear it from me. I got married, Malaina. Two years ago next month." Malaina's eyes widened. "Yep. Not every young filly finds me as homely as you do, you know." She smiled. He went on. "Elizabeth. Elizabeth Johnson. Perty name, ain't it? And she was a vision, darlin'! A vision! Deep brown eyes...so dark you could hardly tell where that little black spot in her eye was. And yeller hair. Yeller as gold and soft as silk. A purty spunky little thing, too. She kept me in line all right." He paused and Malaina began to feel depressed.

"We got married in October. She died in December, darlin'." Malaina gasped and put a hand to her mouth. She couldn't say anything. She couldn't even begin to think of what to say to such a revelation. Baker continued, "Doc Pritchard said her appendix busted. It was all so unexpected...and so fast. It was over before I even knew what was goin' on. Mama's got the weddin' picture up in the attic somewhere if you ever wanna see her."

"I'm sorry, Baker. I had no idea," Malaina whispered, feeling miserable through her tears.

Baker put a finger under her chin and lifted her face to look at him. "Here now! What are you sorry for, sugar?" He took a handkerchief from his shirt pocket and began dabbing her tears. "It's clean, don't worry," he said with a smile and Malaina laughed.

"How devastating for you, Baker. I'm so sorry," she said as she took the handkerchief from him and finished wiping her tears.

"Yes," he said, looking thoughtful. "Sometimes I wonder...was it harder to lose her after only a few months of knowin' and lovin' her...or would it have been harder to love her for twenty-eight years and lose her...like Mama did Daddy?"

An opportunity that Malaina had been waiting for ever since she had come to this family presented itself at that moment. "What happened to your daddy, Baker?"

Baker smiled at her. "Our daddy," he began. "Our daddy was the wisest and handsomest man ever born on this earth."

Malaina smiled as Matthew agreed with a hearty, "You bet your sweet bacon, he was."

Baker went on. "He met Mama durin' the war. He was a Johnny Reb, you know...and Mama was a beautiful, young daughter of a Yankee officer. Mama's family had got caught behind enemy lines in Georgia tryin' to help some relatives escape the burnin'. Daddy found them while on patrol one fine, southern afternoon and helped them escape. It's an awful long story. Get Mama to tell you about it. Anyway, after the war...he kidnapped her and they eloped, moved out west and started havin' us boys. Jackson was the first... and if you wanna know my daddy...know Jackson. He's the spittin' image of Daddy in every way there is."

"That's fer dang sure!" Matthew added firmly and

72

Malaina noticed a smile appear on Mary's face as she looked at him.

"It was three years ago that he died," Baker stated.

"I was still away," Matthew muttered.

Baker nodded. "Daddy was breakin' a horse out in the corral. Mama was out there with me and Jackson watchin'. It was a mean one! Meanest I ever seen to this day. He threw Daddy, which weren't no easy thing in itself...then, before Daddy could stand up, that ol' cuss reared up and planted his front hooves in the middle of Daddy's back. He lived long enough to tell Mama he loved her when she reached him. Then he passed. Jackson slit the thing's throat with that big ol' knife he used to carry." Matthew nodded.

Everyone was silent. After a while Baker sighed heavily. "He was the best husband and daddy I ever seen," he said. He chuckled when he saw the skeptical look on Malaina's face. "Don't let him fool you, darlin'. Jackson is our daddy over and over. And Mama says that Daddy used to try and play tough ol' buzzard, too."

"Mr. McCall was the handsomest old man I ever saw, Malaina," Mary added. "And kind to boot. He never passed the candy counter at Johnson's store without buyin' me a licorice whip. He used to bounce me on his knee when no one was lookin'. I miss him. Everybody misses him."

"We thought Mama was gonna follow him there for a few days. It nearly killed her to lose him," Matthew said. "She keeps all his photographs in her room...to herself. I reckon someday she'll share 'em again."

Malaina sat silent. What loss this family had experienced in the past several years. It was unimaginable to her.

❧

The McCall boys helped the girls down from the buggy and into the general store.

"Hello! Baker! Darlin'! How are you? It's been too long, boy!" a beautiful blonde woman called from behind the store counter.

"Hello, Mrs. Johnson," Baker greeted as the woman rushed out and flung her arms about him.

Malaina recognized the woman from church and guessed that this Mrs. Johnson must be the mother of Baker's Elizabeth.

"And you must be, Annie," she said, offering a hand in greeting.

"Actually," Malaina said, taking the woman's hand, "I prefer to go by Malaina."

"Oh. Forgive me, dear. I could've sworn that Maggie said..."

"The girls are wantin' to make some new dresses for the dance, Mrs. Johnson," Baker interrupted.

Mrs. Johnson smiled and spun around, motioning for the girls to follow. "Oh my, yes! We've got some lovely prints! This way."

After an hour in the general store, Malaina had chosen some lovely cloth for a dress, and learned every bit of new gossip about everyone. Mary and Malaina stepped out of the store into the cool autumn day and began looking for Baker and Matthew.

"I'm sure they're off talkin' horse manure with someone," Mary said grinning.

Malaina smiled. "Well, I guess we'll just sit here and wait." She motioned to a nearby bench.

They had been waiting for a few minutes when a voice penetrated her ears that made Malaina's flesh crawl.

"Well, well, well. If it ain't, Miss Malaina."

Malaina and Mary had been looking at each other while they talked and hadn't noticed the grimy looking man that now stood before them. Malaina looked up and terror struck her. She recognized the man! She didn't know from where, but she knew that he meant her harm.

"What do you want?" she asked bravely.

The man raised his brows sarcastically. "It ain't what I want, missy...and you know it. I've been lookin' for you for weeks now and I'm plum sick of it. You've been the cause of my havin' to be sleepin' on the hard ground for that long."

"I'm sorry, but I've no idea what you're talking about," Malaina mumbled, smoothing her skirt and smiling as Mary stood and walked casually away.

"Oh! My, my, my. Have we misplaced our memory somewhere?" the man said sarcastically. "Now...Miss Malaina...you'll come with me quiet like and we'll take you back to Mr. Collin where you belong."

At the mention of the name Collin, panic gripped

her. "I'm not going anywhere with you," she said firmly and stood to leave.

The man took her wrist roughly in his hand. "Yes, you are! I'm gettin' paid for my time! I have my orders. You're goin' back...alive...or dead. It don't matter to me none," he growled.

Malaina couldn't believe the man was serious in his intentions. But he was. She felt it. She was in danger. She looked around frantically.

"Don't try screamin'," he whispered and she felt something sharp press against her waist. "I mean what I say."

She knew she would rather die than go anywhere with this vermin. She had to think of some way to escape him.

"Come along, Malaina," he growled, and pushed her ahead of himself.

Mrs. Johnson came out of the store just then. She looked at the man oddly. "It was nice to meet you, Malaina. You come visit real soon."

"Yes. I will. Thank you," Malaina said, hoping the woman would realize that something was amiss and send for help somehow.

They began to cross the dusty road and walk toward a horse that was tied outside the saloon.

"Maybe I'll just keep you to myself," the man whispered into her ear. She wanted to vomit at the stench of his breath. "But, even I know better than to cross a man like Mr. Collin." The man returned his knife to its place at his waist. "Now then," he began. "I can still kill you...easily. So just get on this horse and we'll ride away. No one knows enough about you to concern theirselves. I checked on that."

But as the man moved to untie the reins of his horse Malaina ran. She ignored his order to stop and she didn't stop until she was stopped by someone.

"Please, let me by!" she screamed. But when she felt her arms clenched in two powerful hands she looked up and nearly fainted with relief as Jackson's angry expression met her.

"Sorry, mister," the awful man said approaching. "My sister is a little out of her mind. I need to get her home."

Jackson moved to stand in front of Malaina. "She is home, sir. I think you need to mount that dog-ugly horse and ride away."

The man was undaunted. "Look here, mister...I'm takin' that girl with me. And lest you wanna die where you stand...you'll keep your long, ugly nose to yourself."

Jackson spoke to Malaina although he continued to glare at the man. "Now, you run along, darlin'. Baker and Matthew are over at the feed store. You run along."

Malaina didn't move. She didn't want to leave him.

"Malaina," he growled, and she turned and began running toward the feed store. She didn't dare look back, though she could hear them talking in low, angry voices.

A man was coming toward her and he spoke as he neared. "Now, you keep walkin', miss. I'm Sheriff Braddock, I'll help ol' Jackson out. Tell them other two boys what's goin' on, in case Mary didn't find 'em yet."

She felt hope in relief begin to wash over her. The sheriff was there to help Jackson. She slowed her pace to a brisk walk for a moment, but began to run as she spotted the sign marking the feed store. Baker and Matthew were standing outside and came toward her when they noticed her approaching.

"What's wrong, honey?" Baker asked, catching her in his arms.

"A man...he tried to abduct me! To take me back! Jackson...the sheriff...over in front of the saloon," she panted.

"Stay here, Malaina. Go inside and stay here," Baker ordered and they began running.

Malaina stood outside for several moments watching them disappear around the corner.

Mary reached her then, and flung her arms around her. "Oh! Thank goodness! I was so worried! I couldn't find the boys...so I told Sheriff Braddock. I just knew you were done for."

Malaina pulled away from Mary and started running toward the corner that the McCall men had just cleared. The man had a gun! She had just realized it. And Jackson, Baker and Matthew weren't carrying any.

"Malaina! Wait!" Mary called after her.

But Malaina was panic-stricken! He was a vile man. She knew he'd do anything to get her back to Collin.

Just before she turned the corner she heard a gunshot slice the air. Then quickly, another. She stopped for a moment in horror and then rounded the corner.

The vile man was lying on the ground. But, so was Jackson. "No!" she gasped as she slowed to a walk. Baker and Matthew were kneeling down beside their brother and the sheriff was standing over the degenerate.

The sheriff motioned to another man and he came over and felt the villain's neck. Malaina stopped several feet away from the scene. Then she began to shudder with horrific relief as she saw Baker helping Jackson to stand. She stood frozen. Not even registering their conversation.

" Over here, Doc. Big, bad, brother Jackson's been up to no good again," Baker called to the doctor who had just informed the sheriff that the other man was dead.

"It ain't nothin'," Jackson muttered, opening his shirt to examine the wound to his left shoulder.

"Mama will have a livin' fit over this Jackson," Matthew chuckled.

Malaina still stood frozen. She watched as Jackson took off his shirt and held it to the wound. The three walked toward her with enormous grins of triumph plastered across their faces.

Matthew called out to her, "You won't be bothered by him no more, Malaina. Jackson beat the…heck out of him and then after he shot Jack, Sheriff Braddock shot him back. He's done."

"Dang right!" Jackson said, smiling as Baker slapped him on the back.

They stood directly in front of her now smiling

proudly and patting each other all over.

"You think this is funny?" she choked, looking at the shirt Jackson held to his shoulder that was now saturated with his own blood.

"Not at all, sugar," Jackson said. "It just means you're out of danger. From that varmint, anyhow."

"Dang right," Matthew said, smiling at Baker.

Anger began to add itself to the horror that Malaina was feeling. "How can you laugh about this?" she screeched. "He's been shot! You all stand there with your swollen up egos smiling and slapping each other on the back like a bunch of idiots! What is wrong with you?"

They looked back and forth at each other with puzzled expressions.

Then Mary spoke from behind, "Malaina, Jackson probably saved your life...again, I might add. What are you scolding him for?"

Malaina spun around enraged. "He could've been killed, Mary! Killed! That means dead! I should've just gone with the man."

"Now wait a minute..." Jackson growled, taking her arm and turning her to face him. "That's about the most ignorant thing I've ever heard you say. It's a scratch." He smiled down at her.

"It's a bullet, Mr. McCall," she said as tears began to stream down her face.

"So what. I'm sure Doc can dig it out."

Malaina shook her head and let out an hysterical laugh. "Forgive me! How silly of me! I was always under the impression that most folks die from being shot!"

The boys all looked at each other. Then Jackson smiled at her, speaking softly to his brothers. "I know what's the matter with her, fellas. I've got my shirt off again. She always gets so upset when I got my shirt off."

They all three stifled snickering and Malaina's teeth ground each other as rage took over. She moved to slap Jackson, but he caught her hand and twisted it behind her back.

"Excuse us, will you?" he said, smiling at everyone. Then he directed her forcefully into the alley nearby.

"I don't mean to be crude, little miss ruffled up drawers...but that ain't the kind of man that keeps his distance when he's waltzin' with you. Do you get my meanin'?" he said, glaring down into her face.

"Thank you for the information. It's such a surprise," she spat, trying to move past him.

But he pushed her up against the wall, pinning her still with his bloody hand, which had dropped the shirt. "Malaina...don't be ignorant. You know what would've happened if he would've gotten away with you. Now, my brothers and me...we been hurt a lot. And bad. Don't be acting so ridiculous over this."

She felt ill. He had nearly been killed this time, trying to help her.

"It's too much, Mr. McCall. I've got to leave. I've put your family harm's way too often. Please...just lend me the money to leave here," she pleaded, pressing firmly against his chest with her hands as she stared into his face. "I promise that I'll find a way to pay you back."

He let out a heavy breath of aggravation. "Malaina, I don't want to hear that again. If you hate it here...I'll help you out. But I don't think you do. And it would destroy my mama." She looked away. "Do you hate it here, Malaina?" he asked firmly. She didn't answer. He took her face firmly in hand and forced her to look at him. "Do you? Tell me. If you do...I'll send you away."

She looked up into his beautiful green eyes. She loved life with the McCalls, she loved the land, the warm dry air--the smell of peaches cooking into preserves. And most of all she loved him. She knew it like she knew breathing.

"I love...it here, Mr. McCall," she whispered.

He let go of her face and drew in a deep breath. "My name is, Jackson, darlin'. Now...let me pay the doc a visit." And he turned and walked away.

She smoothed her hair back, wiped her cheeks on her sleeve, and walked back into the street as she straightened her skirt. Mary stood there looking at her with a stunned expression.

"I'm fine, Mary. Really," she said. Then she turned to Baker and Matthew who both looked gravely at her. "I'm sorry, Baker...Matthew. It was just such a shocking experience. Thank you so much. You'll never know how much I thank you."

They looked at each other. "Mama is gonna tan our hides, Baker," Matthew said, studying Malaina from head to toe.

"Dang right," Baker added.

Mary began to hug Malaina, but pulled away. "You

boys are in big trouble with Mrs. McCall. You're gonna take Jackson home all shot up and now this," she said, pointing at Malaina.

"What?" Malaina asked.

She looked down at her skirt. It was streaked with blood where she had touched it. She gasped and looked at her hands. They were covered with blood, too. Then she realized that she had smoothed her hair and wiped her cheeks. There was also a large stain on the back of her dress where Jackson had pressed against her while directing her to the alley.

"We're really in the dog house this time," Matthew said.

"Okay, folks. It's all over. Just had us a bad one in town today," Sheriff Braddock called to all the onlookers that Malaina hadn't even noticed. "You all right, miss?" he asked her. She nodded, feeling even more self-conscious now that she was covered in Jackson's blood. "Well, you're mighty lucky you've got good ones like the McCalls for friends," he said, smiling encouragingly at her. Then he left.

"After the doc patches Jackson up...we'll get home and face the music, Malaina. I guess me and Baker should finish up business at the feed store. Give us a holler when he's done," Matthew said as he and Baker began walking away, leaving Malaina and Mary.

"I guess we could visit with Mrs. Johnson some more, Malaina. If you want," Mary said smiling.

Malaina was feeling very weak and shaky. "No, Mary. Let's just sit out of the way for awhile...please.

What am I going to do, Mary?" Malaina asked more to herself than the girl.

"What do you mean?" Mary asked, taking Malaina's hand comfortingly between her own.

"I can't possibly stay here! All I am is trouble to the McCalls. He could've been killed, Mary!"

"He wasn't Malaina. And you've got to realize that this is life out here. People have to be tough, hard, and able to survive."

If it meant people you loved died all around you, then she wasn't sure she wanted to stay. She pressed hard against her temples with her hands. "I've got to remember things, Mary. I've got to!"

They sat in silence for several minutes until Matthew approached them. "Sheriff don't know who that man is, Malaina. Ain't got nothin' with a name about him." He smiled at Mary.

Malaina seemed preoccupied. "His name is Beau Benson and Collin hired him to pursue me after I ran away. I sold a diamond broach that my mother had left to me and the money took me as far as Cripple Creek. Beau tracked me there and had orders to bring me back to New Orleans. He forced me to go with him by holding a gun at my back, but when the stage stopped to change the stage horses, I hid and never got back on. I thought I'd be safe in that small town, I can't remember what one it was, but his brother, Dill, found me. I hit Dill over the head with a log when we were near Cortez. It only stunned him and I started running. He must have fallen unconscious at some point...obviously...because Jackson found me first, didn't he?" She looked over at Mary and Matthew who were staring at her with their mouths wide open.

Matthew regained his senses first.

"Well, who is this Collin feller...and why does he want you? You ain't his wife...are you?" he asked.

"No!" Malaina answered vehemently. "I am not his wife! If nothing else, I know that." Then Malaina's eyes widened in horror. "Matthew! What if I killed Dill? What if I hit him so hard that I killed him?"

Matthew shrugged his shoulders. "If he's dead, he's dead...and that's one less varmint that'll be after you then, ain't it?"

Malaina was shocked to silence at his matter-of-fact answer.

"Here comes Jackson and Baker. Let's get home, girls," Matthew said, offering a hand to each of them.

Jackson looked up and down at Malaina and she made a fruitless effort at smoothing her hair that was matted with dried blood.

He smiled. "Looks like you'll really be needin' that new dress now."

She looked at him intending to respond smartly until she saw the bandages at his shoulder and the sling supporting his arm. Guilt overwhelmed her and tears brimmed in her eyes.

"I'm so sorry," she whispered humbly.

"Ain't no big deal. Ol' Doc just dug it right out a there, slapped on a dressin' and I'm ready for anythin'."

"You better be. Looks like a feller named Dill might

be showin' up one day with the same intentions," Matthew stated.

Malaina looked at him, sickened.

"Who?" Baker asked.

"Seems this ol' boy that the undertaker just drug off has a brother who's workin' for this Collin feller, too. Ain't that right, Malaina?"

Malaina nodded. "I've got to leave here!" she pleaded, looking from one brother to the other.

"You ain't goin' nowhere, darlin'," Baker said, putting an arm around her shoulder. "You're safer with us than anywhere on earth."

"But you all aren't," she said bitterly.

"She keeps askin' me to lend her money to go east. Hey, how come you always ask me, anyway, girl?" Jackson asked, suddenly curious. "Baker and Matthew... they got as much money as me."

She cast her eyes down unable to answer at first.

"Well, it seems to me...she knows me and Matthew want her here no matter what. But you, Jackson…you see...you're a grouchy ol' bear and she figures you want rid of her. Ain't that right, darlin'?"

But she really couldn't answer. Maybe it was really because he was always the one coming to her rescue.

She scowled as a pounding headache started in her head, and lifting her skirts to climb into the buggy that they were all standing before now, she said, "Let's just get back. I feel horrid."

"Bill's over at the blacksmith, Baker. He threw a

shoe this mornin'. You think you could ride him home for me? I'm a little sore."

Baker laughed. "I ain't ridin' that maniac of yours, Jack. We'll tie him to the buggy and lead him home."

Jackson and Matthew looked at each other and laughed.

"Not if you wanna actually get home, Baker. You know he won't have none of that," Matthew said. "Why'd you bring him to town for shoein', Jackson? You usually do all the shoein' at home."

Jackson climbed into the buggy and let out a heavy breath as he settled himself. Malaina knew that the wound hurt him, no matter what he said.

"I threw the shoe on the way to town. Jerry Smithe came over a while after you all left. He said there was a dirty lookin' ol' thing in town askin' about Malaina. I came to see what was goin' on. Now, who's ridin' Bill home? I ain't leavin' him here."

Malaina stood up and hopped down from the buggy. "Me," she stated, walking toward the livery.

"Over my dead body!" Jackson shouted when he realized she was serious.

"Apparently so," she said, looking at his wound.

"You don't wanna ride Bill, Malaina. He's meaner than a sat on yeller jacket!" Matthew warned.

They all thought she was kidding. She kept walking.

"Malaina," Jackson called as he climbed down from the buggy. "Don't be ignorant." He caught up to her, grabbing her arm and spinning her around. She broke his grasp violently.

"I am not one of your horses in need of breaking, Mr. McCall!" She glared up at him and he returned it.

"I'm not so sure about that. And I can break anything," he growled.

Her mouth dropped open at such a vulgar remark and she moved to slap him yet again. And, yet again, he caught her arm with his free hand.

"You are not ridin', Bill. You can't. He won't have no part of it."

She ripped her wrist from his grip. "You can break anythin and I can ride anything. You just don't want anyone else to be able to ride him 'cause it'll detract from your superiority."

His eyes narrowed at her. "Fine. Break your uppity little neck, girl." And he turned and walked angrily away.

As she started for the livery again, she heard Matthew say, "You can't let her ride him, Jack. He'll throw her!"

She couldn't hear Jackson's response of, "No he won't. He likes her."

Bill was already saddled and ready to go. Malaina's heart began pounding furiously, as if the pounding in her head wasn't enough. Everyone stood stone still in the livery as she untied Bill and stood in front of him. What a sight she must be! Covered in Jackson McCall's blood and standing here threatening to ride his stallion that everyone, including her, knew was a wild hair.

"Ma'am. Uh...that's ol' Bill...Mr. McCall's horse. I don't know if you wanna..." a man said approaching.

"Yes. I am aware of that, sir. I intend to ride him

home being that Mr. McCall is injured on my account. And why does everyone here insist on calling every animal 'old' something-or-other," she said irritatedly.

Bill snorted and stomped a hoof. She stroked his nose gently, standing close to his nostrils so that he could smell her.

"Now, Bill...you know me. You're going to let me ride you home, aren't you?"

The horse nodded strongly and stomped again.

Malaina talked to him gently and patted his neck for several more minutes. She felt very self-conscious with everyone gawking at her. Finally, she found the courage and tried mounting him. He moved away neighing the first two attempts, but on the third he only snorted and shook his head.

She eased herself into the saddle and when she had the reins in hand she pressed gently with her heels and he shot out of the livery.

"Bill!" she shouted. But he was already in a dead run through the middle of town. "Calm down. Calm down," she told herself. And she pulled up hard on the reins with every muscle in her body just as she reached the buggy where the others sat waiting for her. The horse reared and came down hard, snorting and stomping the ground. A mother walking in front of the store pulled her small child against her and looked at the wild looking woman was before her.

"She's on ol' Bill!" she heard a man say from the saloon across the street.

And within moments Malaina looked around to see

the entire town emerging from one building or another to look at the spectacle. Bill reared again and stomped around madly.

Baker, Matthew, and Mary looked at her with mouths hanging open and eyes as wide as saucers.

Jackson simply raised his eyebrows and said, "No need to wait for us."

"I won't!" she said angrily, and with a "Ya!" as signal to Bill, she rode off at a mad gallop through town and toward the McCall ranch.

CHAPTER NINE

Riding Bill was exhilarating! Even Malaina's headache seemed cured. The sound of the saddle moving with the horse's rhythmic run consoled her somehow. Bill was indeed a magnificent mount.

"Imagine," she said out loud, "naming an animal like you...Bill!" After a time she slowed him. "You are something else, boy!"

She realized that for the first time today...and it had been a long one...she felt like smiling. The sun was setting and it turned the sky all shades of purples, pinks and oranges. The sunsets were so beautiful in the west! She rode the rest of the way calmly, talking to Bill and trying to think more intently on the memories she had acquired earlier.

"So," she said to the horse as she rode, "I'm from New Orleans, my name is Malaina...Malaina something... and some horrible man named Collin is looking for me. But I don't know why. I can't remember who he is, what he looks like or why he wants me. I can't remember if I have parents, siblings, friends to help me, family. Oh Bill! What will I do?"

As the sun set she rode up to the barn at the McCall ranch. She unsaddled Bill, brushed him for a few minutes, gave him oats and water. Then taking a deep breath, headed for the house.

When she opened the screen door and stepped into the kitchen Maggie turned with a smile to greet her. "Oh, honey! I'm so glad you all are..." The smile left her face as she took in the sight of Malaina, dried blood in her hair, on her face, hands, and dress. Her hair was a mass of wind blown mess and she looked as if she needed a month of sleep.

Maggie turned and put her apron under the pump to wet it and then started wiping Malaina's face. "There's so much blood, Malaina...where are you hurt?" she asked, trying to appear calm, although her quivering voice betrayed her.

Malaina took her hands and smiled at her. "I'm fine, Mrs. McCall. I'm fine. There was some trouble in town...a man tried to take me with him. Jackson stopped him and was shot in the shoulder, but he's fine and they're all on their way home in the buggy just now." She rambled it out as fast as she could, hoping the woman wouldn't panic over the news of a wounded son.

Maggie stared blankly at her for some moments. Then she began wiping the dried blood from Malaina's face once more and asked, "How did you get home?"

Malaina could tell that she was extremely upset so she talked calmly as if nothing whatsoever had happened. "I rode Bill. Jackson was a bit sore," she smiled hopefully at the woman.

Maggie's eyes bugged out like a mouse with its head caught in a trap. "Bill? You rode Bill home?" Then she chuckled. "Now quit your teasin', doll. Who brung you home?"

Malaina smiled. "I rode Bill. He's in the barn. I brushed him down. I think he likes me."

Maggie smiled. "Well, I'll be. What did Jackson have to say to that?"

Malaina began unbuttoning her blouse. "I suspect he wouldn't have let me if he thought there was any danger," she said with a delayed realization.

✌

After she had bathed and put her clothes to soak, Malaina let Maggie brush her hair awhile as she told her the events of the afternoon. Maggie listened attentively until she was finished.

"My stars and garters, child! Who in the world are you?" she commented.

"I wish I knew, Mrs. McCall." Then she turned her pleading eyes to the woman. "Please, I've got to leave here! Don't you see? I'm putting you all in great danger!"

Mrs. McCall cupped the beauty's face in her hands and smiled lovingly. "You're ours now, precious. We won't let you run away."

"But, Jackson was shot today, Mrs. McCall! And I believe this Collin won't stop until he finds me. You've got to help me leave," she begged.

But her hopes were dashed when she heard Jackson's

voice from beyond the screen door. "Oh, now turn off them puppy-dog eyes, Malaina. You ain't goin' nowhere," he said.

The others followed him in and Mrs. McCall went to inspect the wound. Malaina noticed immediately how tired Jackson appeared.

"I'll drive Miss Mary home, Mama...and then milk the ones need milkin'. They oughta be bustin' at the seams by now," Matthew said as Mary followed him outside.

"I'll go start milkin' now," Baker said, kissing his mother, winking at Malaina and leaving.

"I'm goin' to bed, Mama," Jackson said, standing. He began to sway and instinctively Malaina took his good arm and placed it around her shoulder. She was surprised when he didn't resist, but leaned on her for support.

"You know, Mama..." he began, his words slurring together. "I feel a might dizzy."

"He's lost a lot of blood, judgin' by what came home all over you, Malaina. Let's put him to bed," his mother sighed.

The two women helped him down the hall to Baker's room where he had been sleeping since Malaina's arrival. Malaina helped him to sit down on the bed and, since his arm was about her, sat with him.

"Ol' Doc is right good at fixin' 'em up, but he never cleans very well. Stay with him, Malaina. We need soap and water," Maggie said, hurrying out of the room.

When Malaina attempted to stand, she found that

Jackson had his arm clamped tightly about her. She looked up into his face. He was frowning down at her. The heavy beads of perspiration appearing on his forehead worried her.

"Mr. McCall?" she asked tentatively.

He grimaced. "Jackson," he corrected emphatically.

Malaina put a hand to his head and then cheek. He was feverish. "Lay down, Jackson. Do you hear me?" she said, pushing him back.

He still held her firmly and when he did finally relent and lay down, he took her with him.

"Let go, Jackson," she said calmly, pushing against him. He was so strong, even in his present condition.

"You rode ol' Bill, did you? He likes you. I can't begin to wonder why. But he does. I wouldn't have let you ride him otherwise," he mumbled.

"Yes. Yes. Now let me go."

"Ain't you gonna thank me, Miss Malaina? I mean for savin' you again? I think a proper thank you is in order." He was grinning slyly.

She looked directly into his eyes. "Thank you, Jackson. Again."

He closed his eyes and he smiled. "Now kiss me," he said, his speech was even more slurred.

"What?" she gasped and as his arm released her he began to chuckle and she realized that he was fine. A little sore and feverish, but fine all the same.

Within seconds he was breathing slowly and she knew he was asleep. Maggie returned with a basin of warm water and rags.

"My poor baby," she murmured as she began to bathe his face. Maggie looked over at Malaina who was deep in thought as she stared at the wounded man. "That's enough, Malaina!" she demanded. "You're staying right here! If he hadn't of gotten shot it would've been somethin' else. This isn't your fault. I know that it was meant for us to find you. You're ours now." She smiled and cupped the girl's cheek in her hand. "Now, help me clean him up. That doctor! Well, at least he patched him up anyway, huh."

Maggie handed a washcloth to Malaina after she had rung it out. "See if you can get some of that dried blood off his chest. I'll go tell Baker to start bringin' in some clean water. We're gonna need a lot more than a bowl full!" Maggie left the room and Malaina began dabbing at the blood.

She jumped when Jackson said, "I'm your knight in shinin' armor, ain't I, sugar?"

She thought he was still asleep. His eyes were still closed, but he wore a slight grin. "How many times have I saved your bacon now?" he asked. Malaina was very self-conscious about cleaning his bare torso now that she knew he was conscious.

"At least three by my count," she answered, sounding remarkably calm. "All you're lacking is a white horse, I'd say," she finished.

He opened his eyes just a bit to look at her. "Dang mess, ain't it?" he said with a note of irritation in his voice. "I'm so dang tired. Can't seem to keep my eyes open much."

"You need to rest. I don't know why you're even trying to stay awake."

Malaina wished he'd go to sleep. It made her very uncomfortable to have him alert while she was bathing him.

He chuckled lowly. "I'm still waitin' for my kiss."

She rinsed the cloth in the basin, causing the water to go red.

"Stop teasing and go to sleep, Jackson," she ordered.

"I must a found another way of gettin' yer dander up," he mumbled. "Well, all right. I'll just corner you out in the barn one day and collect the debt." And with a final chuckle he fell asleep again.

Maggie returned and could tell Malaina was flustered. "What's wrong, peach?" she asked.

"Your son is a flirt when he's out of his head," Malaina told her.

CHAPTER TEN

The family had discussed Malaina's newfound memories that next evening. But everyone was a long way from solving the puzzle, and life returned to normal. Malaina had become close to Mary and was overjoyed as she watched a new type of friendship sprouting between her friend and Matthew.

Mary would often visit so that she and Malaina could work on their dresses for the Harvest Dance and would somehow end up talking with Matthew as he did the chores. Malaina never said a word about it to either one of them, but decided to wait until they chose to come to her. And so things went along.

One early evening about dusk, Maggie asked Malaina to run and get a hammer out of the barn. Malaina wrapped up in a shawl and headed out to do the errand.

The weather was cool and Malaina was unaccustomed to it. She found it hard to warm herself at times. She guessed it was because she'd always lived in a warm climate. She entered the barn and began rummaging through the toolbox for a hammer.

"Whatcha need?" Jackson asked from behind her. Malaina spun around startled.

"Don't do that! You scared the life out of me," she answered.

"Sorry. What are you lookin' for?" he asked, coming to stand beside her and looking down into the box.

"A hammer. There's a nail out of one of the kitchen chairs and your mama wants to fix it."

Jackson put down the brush he'd been using on Bill and began digging in the box. Malaina noticed that he was, once again, without a shirt.

"It's freezing out here, Jackson! How can you run around half dressed like that."

He chuckled. "I ain't a bit cold. I hope you start gettin' a little more used to this weather. It gets ten times worse than this, darlin'."

Malaina shivered involuntarily. "Really?" she asked. The thought was not at all comforting. "Well, you should put some clothes on anyway," she stated as he stood handing her a hammer.

"Why?" he asked with his sly grin spreading across his lips.

"It's indecent. That's why. Have you not one shred of modesty in your being, Jackson?" she answered.

"Not a shred," he whispered.

"I think you do it to show off," she mumbled to herself.

"You do?" he asked, raising his eyebrows as his smile broadened. He took a step toward her and she stepped backward bumping up against the barn wall.

"Yes," she answered, trying to appear unrattled. He put one hand against the wall behind her and leaned close to her face.

"Why do you think that I'm showin' off when I work without a shirt on, Malaina?" he asked almost in a whisper.

She opened her mouth to answer but none came.

"What, exactly, do you think I'm tryin' to show off?"

"Your...Your..." she stammered.

He raised his eyebrows. "My what?"

She gritted her teeth and took a deep breath. "Yourself!" she answered.

He chuckled and put the other hand on the wall. "You mean, my body. Is that what you mean?"

She felt herself begin to blush and was horrified that she should.

"It sure ruffles your feathers whenever we get on this here subject, girl," Jackson said, still smiling slyly at her and moving closer.

"We have a name for men like you where I come from," she told him, blushing a deeper crimson.

"Really?" he asked, raising his eyebrows. "And what would that word be, Malaina? Rounder? Cad? Or maybe it's more like the perfect lover."

Her eyes widened at his conceit. "You are impossible!" she exclaimed.

He chuckled and moved so close to her that she felt the warmth of his breath on her forehead. "Why don't you try me out and see for yourself," he mumbled, taking her by the shoulders and locking eyes with her.

"You're a beast!" she scolded, though it came out in more of a whisper than mean and harsh as she had meant it to sound.

"I'm callin' in your debt now, Miss Malaina. Here and now," he whispered just before he kissed her.

Malaina struggled for a split second, but as the feel of his sensual mouth on hers engulfed her, she was swept away. It lasted only a few seconds, but it was long enough to prove to her that he had been right about himself. It took every bit of restraint in her being for her not to wrap her arms around his magnificent form and passionately return his kiss. When he broke the kiss, she glanced up at him and then away quickly.

"You're a shameless flirt," she whispered as she moved past him.

"Not really," he said, picking up a pitchfork and giving the cow some hay. "You're just so funny when you're embarrassed that I can't help it." She heard him chuckling as she walked quickly toward the house.

❧

"It must really be nippy out there. You're as red as a beet!" Maggie said as Malaina entered kitchen.

Actually she felt a little too warm. "Yes. I guess I'm not used to this cool weather."

Maggie smiled as Malaina handed her the hammer.

"I've just now remembered where I put that lace that I thought might look nice on the collar of your dress, love," Maggie said, sitting down on the floor and preparing to fix the chair. "Now, up in the attic there's a whole load of mess, so watch your step. There's four or five trunks up against one wall and I think I laid that lace in the top one. Go have a look will you? It's white with a pretty design woven in. Run along now."

Malaina smiled as she pulled down the ladder to the attic and began climbing.

The attic was stuffy and she was glad she'd brought a lamp with her because it was pitch dark inside now that the sun had set. She began looking around.

"Mess?" she spoke out loud. "Treasure!"

There were old harnesses, an old dress form in one corner, and other wonderful things piled around. She quickly spotted the trunks up against the wall and went over eagerly. They weren't, however, piled up the way Maggie had described, but rather all of them were sitting on the floor. She shrugged her shoulders and opened one.

It wasn't the correct trunk, obviously, but her curiosity was peaked as she spied a uniform of some sort lying in it. She lifted it slightly. It was familiar. Not Confederate or Northern from the war, but still very familiar. A photograph fell out of the folds and as she held it up she recognized the uniform worn by the man in the photograph.

"West Point?" she muttered as she stared down at the handsome face of Baker dressed in the uniform and standing in front of the sign that greeted all visitors to the institution. How dashing he looked! She couldn't resist looking deeper into the trunk. Below the uniform was another photograph. A very large one, and she knew at once that this was his wedding photo.

Baker looked so handsome dressed formally. Next to him stood Elizabeth. She had been a unique beauty, just as he had described her. They looked so blissful and Malaina felt as if something had pierced her heart. She quickly replaced everything and shut the trunk. She dusted the top off to reveal a brass nameplate and read, "Baker Robert McCall."

She moved to the next trunk and dusted the nameplate. "Matthew Robert McCall." And the next. "Jackson Robert McCall. All named after their daddy, Robert," she said to herself. Jackson's trunk was locked. She wondered what secrets it held.

The next trunk looked much older and much more worn. She dusted it off. Instead of a fancy nameplate, the name was carved into the wood. "Robert Jackson McCall," she read and she knew that she dared not open it.

Malaina moved to another trunk and lifted the lid. Sure enough, the lace was there. She quickly grabbed it, shut the trunk and hurried down the ladder. She felt as if she'd been eavesdropping somehow.

"Did you find it?" Maggie called from the kitchen.

"Oh, yes! It's lovely, Mrs. McCall. I can't possibly use this! It's just too lovely." Malaina exclaimed.

She entered the kitchen to find the three men and their mother sitting at the table waiting for her. How long had she been up there?

"I'm sorry. I had no idea we were this close to dinner," she said, taking her seat. Her confidence had returned and she smiled sarcastically at Jackson and said, "I'm glad you decided to actually dress before dinner."

Maggie rolled her eyes. "Jackson McCall! It is entirely too cold to be working without a shirt now. And I want you to start wearing your long johns!"

Jackson smiled at his mother. "Better watch your backs boys. Little Miss Proper Pants is a tattler."

"Jackson!" his mother scolded, trying to hold back a snicker.

Baker started the dinner conversation. "I saw horse tracks out by the north pasture today. Ten riders, I'd say. Unshod."

Matthew and Jackson looked at their brother and all smiles faded.

"It's gettin' colder...they're hungry," Matthew said.

"I'm sure they're hungry all right. But I'm wonderin' what for," Baker said directly to Jackson.

"Quit talkin' over my head boys. Is it Black Wolf?" Maggie asked and Malaina felt as if her blood had turned to ice.

"Can't think of any other ten unshod ponies 'round here, Mama," Baker said. "Don't worry, though. As long as it's the cattle their eyein' up I ain't worried."

They all looked at Malaina suddenly. "What? What are you lookin' at me for?" she asked, beginning to shiver.

"Did Mary come visit today?" Matthew asked changing the subject.

"No," Malaina said flatly.

"You girls only got a couple of days to finish them

new duds. I thought you'd be sewin' your little fingers blue by now," he said.

"We're nearly finished," Malaina commented, still preoccupied by the previous conversation.

"Well, I can't wait for that dance!" Baker said smiling. "It's been a long time since we done anything sociable around here."

"Dang right," Jackson said. "I saw that little Justine Smithe in town last week. She sure turned out purty." Malaina looked at him quickly and then away.

"Here we go," Maggie said. "Sizin' up the goods already," she giggled.

"Well, you want grandbabies before you're a hunderd don't you, Mama?" Baker asked.

"Oh, yes!" she answered.

Malaina was feeling nauseated. She hadn't considered that Jackson might be flirting with other women there.

"Ol' Jackson better beware this year, Mama. I heard that the Widow Thompson still has her eyes on him," Matthew said, laughing.

"Older women is like fine wine, little brother. Better and better with age," Jackson said.

"How would you know, Jack? You ain't never had fine wine," Baker teased.

Everyone laughed and Malaina even managed a smile.

Baker continued, "Well, I got my eye on that little Susan Adams. She's got that purty auburn hair and her eyes are matchin'."

"Oh, she *is* lovely!" Maggie added.

"Well, I know little brother Matt here will have his hands full enough with our own Mary...so who is gonna chaperon Malaina?" Baker asked.

"I don't need a chaperon," she stated.

They all looked at each other with raised eyebrows.

"You most certainly do!" Maggie exclaimed.

"The men 'round here ain't much on manners and the proper ways...as you well know, darlin'," Jackson said with a wink.

"Well, as you know, Jackson...I am most certainly aware of that. And I still don't need a chaperon."

"She thinks I'm a neked barbarian, boys. She caught me with my pants down today...well, actually with my shirt off...and then she went on in here and told Mama," Jackson said.

"That does seem to upset her every time, don't it," Matthew snickered.

"It's a good thing it weren't with your pants down, I guess," Baker said and as they busted into laughter Maggie scolded.

"All right, boys! That's enough. You quit your teasin'! Just 'cause Malaina has some modesty don't mean you can give her grief about it every day of the week. I'll keep Malaina company if and when she ever has time on her hands. I'm sure those young men in town will snatch her clean away from us."

Jackson snickered. "Naw. She won't like any of them boys. They'll all be wearin' shirts." Maggie sighed in exasperation as the three boys broke into peels of laughter.

107

Even Malaina had to laugh at their teasin'. They all cared for her in some way, she knew. Even Jackson. Otherwise he wouldn't tease her all the time the way he did.

∾

Two days before the dance Mary and Malaina were in the north pasture. "Well, you got waltzin' down perfect. I guess you all waltz down south at least. But you still haven't got any reels or anything. So, let's get started," Mary said.

Malaina had awakened in the night several days before realizing that dancing out west might be very different than dancing in the south. So she had asked Mary about it and found that the assumption was, indeed, correct. As a result, Mary and Malaina had been sneaking off to the north pasture and practicing.

"I don't know what the point is anyway, Mary. I don't know anyone here. I'll just be the perfect example of a wallflower, I'm sure," Malaina commented.

"Don't be silly, Malaina! I swear all the men in town take to droolin' like dogs whenever you're around. Let's try the two-step. We do it more than waltzin' anyway."

Malaina found it very easy to learn. It was similar to the waltz and the gentleman held you the same way. As they practiced they talked.

"You mean the women don't wear gloves when?" Malaina asked in surprise.

"Of course not, Malaina," Mary sighed. "You actually have to put your bare hand in his bare hand," she mocked.

"Well," Malaina began again, "does the gentleman at least put a handkerchief between his hand and your waist?"

Mary laughed and Malaina spun around when she heard Jackson laughing as well. There he stood, in the cool October weather wearing boots, pants, a hat, well-worn gloves--and no shirt.

"You beat all, girl. I swear," he said.

"What are you laughing at, Jackson? It's the proper way," she told him.

Jackson took Mary in traditional waltzing form. "Not out here it ain't, Malaina. Looky here! Mary's dancin' with a half neked man and he ain't got a hanky at her waist." Mary and Jackson began laughing so hard that they doubled over.

"You are impossible!" Malaina giggled. It probably did seem rather outlandish to them.

"Now come here. I'll teach you dancin'," Jackson said, motioning to her to join him. Malaina shook her head slightly and stepped back. It would be too much! Too close to him. He'd sense how she felt about him. She was sure.

"Oh, go on, Malaina. I get mixed up trying to lead," Mary said as Jackson removed his gloves and threw them aside, motioning to her again.

"Chicken?" he teased. And with that she placed her hand in his. He tipped his hat back, put his other hand at her waist pulling her against him.

"This close?" she asked shocked.

"Yes, ma'am," he said smiling. "But only with me."

Mary giggled. As Jackson began to lead Malaina in an instructive two-step, Mary counted.

This was indecent! Malaina could feel the muscles in his thighs against her own, her chest was flush with his.

"This isn't proper, Jackson!" she exclaimed, trying to pull away.

"You gotta feel where I'm leading you, Malaina," he chuckled.

"Oh, believe me, I feel where you're leading me, Mr. McCall. Does the word corruption ring a bell?" she said nervously.

Mary giggled.

"Oh relax, Malaina. Mary's standin' right there. I ain't gonna do nothin' improper," he said. And in a few moments when she had mastered the step, he did, indeed, hold her out away from him a bit.

"Of course, the other men at the dance will have their shirts on...so it may not be as fun as it was with me," he teased.

She shoved him away. "You're horrid," she said, turning and stomping away. "Let me know when you're finished being corrupted, Mary, and we'll talk," she called back over her shoulder.

"I'm comin' too, Malaina," Mary said, waving to Jackson and catching up to her.

"He is impossible," Malaina sighed.

Mary smiled. "He makes people laugh, and feel special and happy," Mary said.

Malaina smiled. "Yes. He does," she had to agree.

❦

That night when they all sat down at dinner, the boys were trying to control their snickering.

"All right," Maggie said at last. "What is it?"

"Jackson and Malaina were dancin' out in the north pasture half naked today, Mama," Matthew said and they all broke into laughter.

Maggie looked at Malaina who had gone white. "Boys tease, darlin'. Just let it roll like water off a duck and you'll be fine. Now, you boys act your age. Poor girl is gonna be half mad before you're done with her. And Jackson...you start wearin' your shirt! It's nearly winter out there."

"Yes, Mama," he answered when he could at last take a breath.

CHAPTER ELEVEN

Malaina felt as if she'd swallowed a cavern full of bats as they drove to the dance through the cool October evening. It was so delightful, though. Like a dream! Every time they passed a neighboring farm, the family would fall in line behind the others and everyone joined in singing songs together all the way to town. It was a safe, friendly feeling and Malaina reveled in it. Matthew had taken a separate cart, because he was escorting Mary and her parents. But Malaina road in the back of the buggy with Baker, while Jackson and Maggie were in front.

The barn on the Smithe ranch was decorated with shining Jack-O-Lanterns, scarecrows and other harvest type things. Several men were standing on a bunch of wooden crates that had been pushed together playing fiddles and other instruments. One man was even blowing on a jug. Malaina thought it very odd.

People were already dancing and Baker led Malaina to the floor. She was overcome with nerves for a moment until she realized that everyone was simply having a good time. Most of the men looked like monkeys jumping around or were as awkward as Ol' Root would be dancing. Baker, however, was a very proficient dance partner and made her feel more relaxed. Soon she was laughing and feeling as if she never wanted to leave.

The punch and refreshments were delicious and Malaina found many familiar faces to chat with. The only things that dampened her spirits were the moments when she would see Jackson smiling charmingly down into the face of an adoring, lovely girl. Once he caught her staring at him and winked at her. She turned away quickly, mortified. She caught bits and pieces of conversation among the women and girls and the subject always seemed to be the McCall boys, especially Jackson.

One older woman was flirting shamelessly with Jackson and Malaina summized that this must be the Widow Thompson. He was as polite and charming with her as he was with the others. He hadn't once asked Malaina to dance after an hour and she felt as if she'd been slapped in the face. She was sure that she was the only one he hadn't danced with.

Malaina had just finished a cup of punch and was setting it down when Jackson came to stand beside her. He pulled his pocket watch from its home in his pocket and eyed it closely. "Hhmmm. I believe...yes...this is my dance with you, Malaina. Would you mind?" He had the familiar mischievous look about him.

"Very well," she said, cautiously placing her hand in his.

Just then the fiddler shouted. "All right folks. Quiet

down...quiet down now. It's that time of the year again. We're all celebrating a good and prosperous crop this year! Some folks do this as a tradition to bringin' in the New Year! But we do it at the Harvest Dance!" Whoops and cheers went up from the crowd. "That's right! It's turn down the lamps time. The Kissin' Waltz for lovers!" And the crowd continued to whoop and holler as the lights dimmed.

Malaina looked up at Jackson in complete astonishment. She tried to pull her hand from his.

"You said, 'Very well.' Remember? Now be a lady and dance with your ol' improper pal!" he said, pulling her toward the dance floor.

Malaina looked around. There was Matthew with Mary, Baker with a lovely auburn haired girl. Even Maggie was dancing with a jolly looking older man.

"See, sugar...it's all in fun and completely harmless," Jackson said smiling. He no longer wore his mischievous grin. Simply a friendly smile.

Malaina relaxed and smiled up at him. "You like to...to..." she began.

"Ruffle your pin feathers?" he finished.

"Yes," she said.

"That I do. You're different, you see. Most girls, they just get all giggly and know I'm flirtin'...but you get soooo upset! It's very entertainin'."

"Who is this Justine person you're interested in?" she asked. "I don't believe I've been able to put my finger on her this evening."

"Who?" He looked sincere.

"This Justine girl that you think is so lovely."

He smiled as realization hit him. "Oh! Justine. She is a cute little gal." He pulled her to him suddenly. "See that little brown-haired girl right behind us. That's Justine."

Malaina felt unwell as she looked at the girl. She was a living doll. "Oh," she said.

"Have you found the man of your dreams tonight, darlin'?" he asked smiling.

She had. He was holding her in his arms at that very moment. "No," she answered.

"Well, then, I guess I'll just have to do." Her heart threatened to leap from her bosom. How she wished he wouldn't tease about such things.

"I can't thank your family enough," she said, trying to distract him from their current conversation. "Thank you, too, Jackson. For bringing me here. It's like heaven."

"Oh...you're more than welcome. It's a good time havin' you around to tease. And you do wonders for Mama."

Just then Baker and his partner danced up next to them.

Baker leaned over and whispered, "Better put a little space between you two, Jackson. You'll make our little Malaina nervous." He winked at her.

Jackson whispered a response. "I figure if I wanna really impress her and make her feel right at home...I better be strippin' my shirt off here pretty quick." Jackson and Baker suppressed snickers.

"Well, Jackson…are you gonna?" Baker asked.

"Dang right! You gonna?" Jackson replied.

"Dang right!" Baker said smiling.

Malaina was curious. "What are you two going to do?" she asked.

Jackson seemed to listen intently to the music for a moment, then he whispered, "Well, you see, darlin'… this here's called the Kissin' Waltz."

"Yes," she said, still not understanding.

"Well, you see," he continued, "it's called that for a reason." She waited for him to tell her the reason. He grinned slyly and she began to feel nervous again. "Well, here in a minute…they're gonna blow out all the lamps…and between the time they blow 'em all out and the time it takes to get 'em all re-lit…well…everyone who wants to gets to do some kissin'."

It took only a moment for the meaning of what he was saying to sink completely in. Malaina's eyes widened and she gasped as she understood.

At that moment the fiddler yelled, "All right, boys… blow 'em out and light 'em up!" And everything went dark.

The last thing she saw was Jackson's sly smile and the first thing Malaina felt him do was wrap an arm tightly around her waist, pulling her against his powerful body. Her heart pounded furiously as he slid a hand caressively up her arm and then cupped her chin. When Jackson's lips touched hers tentatively at first, her entire body erupted with goose bumps. He kissed her harder, pulling her tightly to him with both arms about her.

Malaina surrendered. She let her hands slide over his strong chest and up over his shoulders. She pulled herself even more tightly against him. She sensed that the room was beginning to lighten and, realizing the passion of their kiss when she felt his tongue touch her upper lip, she broke the embrace.

She was grateful that Jackson held her for just a brief moment before releasing her, for her knees surely would've given way under her weight. She didn't look at him at first, but looked around the room to see who might have witnessed their kiss. A wave of relief flooded her being as she realized that every other woman on the dance floor was as bright a blush as she was.

"I gotta trap you in the dark more often, darlin'," Jackson said leading her from the dance floor.

"You're worse than any sailor I've heard of," she said, trying to steady her breathing. After he had pinched her cheek affectionately, he sauntered off, leaving her still blushing.

"You keep him in line, love," Maggie chuckled. "He can be mighty flirtatious at these get-togethers."

Malaina blushed an even deeper shade of crimson. "Yes. Flirtatious. I need some air." And she gave Maggie's arm a loving squeeze before heading outside.

Malaina was still a little stunned by the incident and didn't hear a man come in and announce, "I just seen Black Wolf and his varmints ridin' up this way!"

She took her coat from the hook on the wall and went out behind the barn. She was greatly surprised when she saw large snowflakes falling the thin layer of snow already on the ground.

She apologized as she tripped over the feet of a couple that were cuddled up on a hay bale sparking. The thought went through her mind that she wished it were she and Jackson cuddled up on that hay bale.

Walking a good fifty feet from the barn, Malaina wrapped her arms tightly about herself, and drew in a deep breath of crisp Autumn air that was signaling the onset of winter. How she had grown to love it here! The dry air, pink sunsets, the sound of the locust in the elms and willows. And now, the silent beauty of frost and snow falling to earth. Whatever she couldn't remember about her life so long ago in Louisiana, she knew that this was infinitely better.

She whirled around when she heard the girl that sat in her sweetheart's embrace behind her scream. Her hand flew to her mouth in horror as she came face to face with the flaring nostrils of Black Wolf's brutal horse.

"Come with Black Wolf!" he commanded and she shook her head and tried to run past him toward the barn.

Black Wolf reached down, catching her arm. In the next moment, she was lying on her stomach watching the horse's hooves gallop away beneath her.

She heard shouting. It seemed to be the Renegades, but Malaina was sure she heard other voices from the barn.

"Help me!" she tried to scream. But the mad race

of the horse made it nearly impossible for her to get a breath.

For several minutes she was too gripped with fear and panic to react. But then her instincts to survive, which had saved her once before, championed her and she began to struggle.

"Do not move. I will kill you," Black Wolf commanded.

She stopped momentarily, but when Black Wolf looked over his shoulder, shouted at the others and kicked the flanks of his horse to push him faster, she knew that they were being pursued. He wouldn't have time to kill her if she could just fall off.

They came to a creek and Black Wolf's horse faltered. As Black Wolf fought to steady the animal, Malaina pushed herself from the horse and into the water.

It was painfully cold! Like wading in liquid ice, and it only took a matter of seconds for her arms and legs to begin numbing. The snow was falling heavily now and it was hard to see through it.

She heard Black Wolf's blood curdling yell and turned to see his horse fighting the water as it struggled toward her. When he reached out to grab her again, Malaina flung herself down into the freezing water and his torturous grasp overshot her. She stood up shivering and watched as he turned his horse back around for another attempt. Malaina knew that she couldn't endure going under that water again! But she had to, and slipped through his fingers, which tore at her dress, ripping out the back of the bodice.

She was freezing, disoriented. But she heard gunshots and wiped the icy water from her eyes. Several men from the barn had reached the renegades and were shooting at them. Two renegades fell into the water and their blood stained it red. The others began using arrows and knives to defend themselves. Malaina screamed as she saw an arrow hit a man in the shoulder. Then she dropped on her knees, sinking into the frigid water as she recognized the wounded rider. Jackson!

He pulled up on his reins and Malaina watched helplessly as Black Wolf started toward him shouting and readying a weapon that looked like a small hatchet. She stood again, shouting Jackson's name as she watched Black Wolf getting closer. As Black Wolf reached him, Jackson pulled the arrow from his own body and speared the renegade through the heart. Black Wolf fell into the water and Jackson, having lost his balance, followed him.

The remaining renegades retreated and the other men followed. Jackson shoved Black Wolf's corpse aside as he waded through the icy water toward Malaina.

"Come on," he called, motioning to her to walk to him.

"I can't," she forced out in a whisper. "I don't think my legs will move." She felt panic rising in her chest. Her jaws were clenched tightly together because of the cold. "Help me!" she called, trying to extend an arm toward him. Then her knees buckled and her brain began to feel numb. She began to crawl toward him through the icy water.

When Jackson reached her, he fell to his knees panting. "Stay awake, Malaina! You're gonna have to save me first if I'm gonna save you later," he said through chattering teeth. He looked around and finding no help, drug her to ground. The snow was already several inches deep and coming down heavier than ever.

"Listen to me," he said, taking her face roughly in his hand as he fumbled with his pants pocket. "I got hit by an arrow. Now, ol' Black Wolf poisons the tips once in a while. If he has this time...it didn't go deep at all, but if it gets any further into my blood...if it's even there...anyway, it's probably a good thing that I'm frozen to the bone. It'll stop my blood from rushin' around as fast." He withdrew a pocketknife from his pocket at last, and flipped it open. "Make an X mark over the wound and then suck out the blood there," he said.

Malaina didn't even feel cold anymore. "What?" she whispered in disbelief.

Jackson shook her by the shoulders and his voice sounded angry. "Do it! You heard me! Else we'll both die, girl!"

With trembling hands she took the knife. Her fingers were blue and she could hardly hold it steady. He tore his shirt away revealing the wound.

"Hurry up, Malaina!" he yelled. The injury was just under his collarbone and the flesh already looked slightly torn there.

"I don't need the knife," she said, realizing the fact.

"Fine. Just hurry," he commanded. She looked up

at him. "Malaina! Don't get shy on me now. Do you wanna die out here?"

Taking a deep breath, Malaina put her mouth over the wound and sucked hard. Jackson's skin was as cold as the water, and she nearly gagged as warm, salty blood flooded her mouth for the first time.

"Spit it out!" he yelled. She did and repeated the process several times. "Does it taste strange?" he asked suddenly. She wrinkled her brow and looked up at him at such a ridiculous question. "Is there a bitter taste or is it just salty?" he asked.

"Salty," she said, spitting. He held her away from him, reached down, lifted up her soaking dress, and used its hem to wipe her mouth then his wound.

"Come on," he panted. "I know where we are and we better find shelter. This ain't no flurry."

Malaina couldn't move her legs at first. She was frozen stiff, but once they started walking through the snow she began to feel warm and drowsy.

"Don't knock out on me, girl," Jackson said as he began pulling her.

It wasn't very long before they both collapsed into an opening in a large rock formation. It was so dark she couldn't see anything but its outline and the snow. The wind had begun to blow more fiercely by the time they entered the cave.

"Someone is lookin' out for us. I can't believe it," Jackson mumbled.

Malaina could hear him banging around and suddenly a flicker of light pierced the blackness. He came walking back toward her holding an oil lamp.

"Me and Baker...used to play in here when we was boys. It was our hideout. When we got older, we figured it would be a good place to weather out a bad storm and we always kept supplies in it, for sentimental reasons I guess. But farther back there's blankets and such."

"It's okay," Malaina said sleepily. "I'm warmin' up already."

Jackson frowned and put an icy hand to her face. "Come on. We better hurry," he said, pulling her to her feet and starting back into the shelter of the cave.

The cave turned and ran into a dead end twenty feet back where the wind could no longer reach them. Malaina watched drowsily as Jackson began to build a fire in the middle of the room.

"See...there's a hole up top. Wind don't come in, but the smoke goes out." The fire burned orange quickly and he sighed, relieved. "Malaina? Wake up," he demanded as she began to lay down and close her eyes.

"I'm fine now, Jackson. I'm warming up nicely," she said, feeling like she couldn't fight sleep any longer.

"No you ain't, girl. You're freezin' to death!.Now get up!" he yelled, pulling her to her feet. "Don't go to sleep yet...I don't know if I've got the strength to get those clothes off of you by myself!" he said as he removed the remains of his own torn shirt.

Malaina's eyes widened at these words and she even took several steps back.

"Get 'em off," he ordered as he began to strip off his pants.

"You're teasing, of course," she whispered.

"Not a bit, and I don't have time for your proper fussin' now," he said as he stepped out of his pants and boots and lumbered toward her.

"I'll dry out soon, Jackson. It won't take long," she said, smiling nervously as he reached her.

"Yes, it will, Malaina," he said, shoving her aside and opening an old trunk that was up against one cave wall. She sighed with relief as she watched him rummaging through the trunk throwing out blankets, wearing only his red underwear, which he'd sadly mutilated by cutting off the top.

She smiled with relief. "For a minute there I thought you were going to," but her smile faded when Jackson straightened and turned around studying a completed pair of long johns.

"Take 'em off...or I will," he stated, his eyes piercing through her.

Every part of her was frozen. Her fingers were so blue and numb now that she wasn't sure she could if she had the intention of doing so.

"Now," he growled, and she automatically began to step out of her drenched petticoats. He tossed the long johns on the ground at her feet and turned around. "Now, don't you be peepin', girl. I gotta get out of these as well," he said, rummaging through the trunk again. She whirled around with her back to him, mortified.

"You're wanting me to put these on?" she asked.

"They'll just get wet...I'm soaked clear through to my underthings."

She heard the tearing of cloth and he said irritatedly, "I wasn't meaning for you to wear your 'underthings' underneath 'em. Everything that is wet comes off Malaina. Now hurry it up! I ain't gonna look 'til you're ready."

She wanted to cry. What indecency! She quickly stripped everything off of her frozen and now fevered body and put on the awkward men's underwear.

"Finished?" Jackson sighed impatiently.

"Yes," she answered timidly as she pushed up the incredibly long sleeves and legs and checked the trap door to make sure the buttons were secured.

"Move," he ordered as he began laying an old bear skin and blankets on the floor next to the fire. He had torn away the top to the dry long johns that he had put on himself. He worked frantically and kept looking up at her with concern engraven across his face. "Lay down here," he said, pointing to the primitive resting place.

"Gladly," she said as she began to feel dizzy and very hot.

But as Malaina lay down on the rugs she began to shake uncontrollably. Her teeth knocked together and her muscles were so tensed that they pained her. "What are you doing?" she asked as Jackson lay down next to her and pulled a blanket over them.

"You're gonna freeze to death if we don't get your body warmed up. Don't give me any trouble about this,

Malaina. It's necessary if you want to live." As he tried to pull her against him she put her hands on his chest to prevent it. "Malaina. Don't fight me," he growled. She looked up into his eyes and began to shake even harder. She pulled her arms tightly to her chest and let him pull her against his warm body.

Immediately Jackson's teeth began to chatter and Malaina heard him swear under his breath. "You're like ice," he whispered. He held her against him, and panted into her wet hair. "Dang!" she heard him mumble as he put a leg over hers. "You're frozen!"

She felt something warm and moist on her cheek. "You're bleeding!" she exclaimed.

Jackson said nothing and simply reached behind them and produced his pocketknife. He held the blade in the flames of the fire for several seconds. Then he released Malaina, sat up and drove the hot knife into the wound. The look of pain on his face was too much for her. Malaina was unconscious.

CHAPTER TWELVE

Malaina's eyes felt dry as she forced them open. She could still hear the wind whipping about outside the cave. How long had she been asleep? She gradually became aware that her hand and one arm were lying on Jackson's chest, which rose and fell in slow rhythm as he slept. He was lying on his back and her upper body was flush with his. She felt one of his hands resting on her back and she could see the other holding hers where it lay on his massive chest. She was no longer shaking but she felt oddly warm and still dizzy.

Slowly, she raised her head and when Jackson's hand slid from her back, he didn't even stir. She slipped her hand from beneath his and sat up. The fire was burning out so she got up, went to the wood pile and selected wood to stoke the fire with. She could tell it was very cold in the cave, but she felt almost hot, so assumed that she was with fever still.

After she had built up the fire and refreshed her dry mouth with some melted snow that stood in a bucket near them, Malaina sat down next to her sleeping champion. Jackson's breathing was still slow and rhythmic. He stirred slightly and afterward his hands rested on his stomach.

As Malaina studied his rough, calloused hands her attention was drawn to the new wound. It looked horrifying! Dried blood caked the area, and the black from the heated knife caused her to shiver. There had been no doctor to stitch it neatly closed and she knew it would leave a rough scar. She noticed, too, the other scar just above this one. The one he had received at yet another attempt at saving her.

She brought her hands up to cover her face as the tears of guilt and thankfulness erupted. Malaina cried quietly for several moments, looking at the damage she'd caused to his magnificent form.

"All you lack is the white horse. Every little girl dreams of a knight coming to her rescue, you know," she whispered as she sobbed quietly. "I'm so sorry."

He looked so sweet. Like a little boy, she thought. His hair was tousled and he slept so soundly. She wiped her tears and stood up again, taking a deep breath. "I must look a mess!" she whispered, trying to change her train of thought. She picked up the top of the long johns that Jackson had mutilated and dipped a sleeve into the bucket of water. She bathed her face and then turned her attention to her shoulder. While lying with him, the blood from Jackson's wound had stained her own shoulder. She slipped the red flannel off of her shoulder and removed her arm holding the garment at her chest. She wiped away the blood that had soaked through the cloth and onto her own skin. The thought of again being covered in the blood of the man she was in love with caused the tears to reappear.

"I'm so sorry," she whispered.

"For what?" The sound of his voice so unexpectedly startled her and she spun around so quickly that she nearly lost the grip on her underwear. He stood before her, clutching his own garment at the waist. These underwear had no drawstring rigged up by his mother to secure them.

There he stood...only half dressed, looking just like the magnificent lover that he'd teased her about.

"I'm sorry for nearly getting you killed yet again," she said, looking down at her exposed shoulder and rubbing it harder with the wet cloth.

"I figure...you'll be the death of me yet, girl," he said. But no smile crossed his face.

All the guilt she felt for his injuries exploded. She threw the wet cloth at him and burst into tears. "You are so cruel!" she screamed in a tear-choked whisper. She tried to move past him but he caught her arm.

"Lay back down," he ordered. "You're still very flushed and hot."

"I'm fine," she growled, but the painful chills were returning.

"I said...lay down, Malaina," he commanded through gritted teeth.

"I just want to walk around for a..." but the dizziness hit her and she stumbled. Reflexively she reached out for him to steady herself. He caught her with one arm and pulled her against him. She let go her grip on her garment and fell against him, weakened. Subsequently the other side of her garment slipped down and both of her shoulders were exposed.

"I think I had better lay down," she mumbled. She felt him lay her gently down on the bearskin again and she drifted off to sleep almost immediately.

❦

When Malaina woke next, she was again lying on Jackson's torso as he slept. She raised herself and sat looking at him. The hand that had been clutching his underwear had relaxed and she hoped silently that he wouldn't move, otherwise she would be embarrassed to utter death.

She studied his wound for a moment and it looked like he had escaped infection. "Oh! It is so hot in here!" she whispered to herself, slipping her other arm out of the long johns and tying the sleeves across her chest in order that the garment should not slip off. With shoulders and arms exposed, she lay back down and tried to rest. She wiped the perspiration from her forehead and frowned. Sitting up again she muttered quietly, "It is *so* hot!"

"Well, don't slip anymore of them longies off...it's too hard on a man," Jackson mumbled.

Malaina looked questioningly at him. His eyes were closed. She was sure. She bent close to his face and whispered, "Are you awake?"

He smiled. "Of course I'm awake."

"Well, it's very hot in here," she stated irritatedly.

"You're tellin' me," he mumbled.

"What?" she asked, but he only grinned with his eyes still closed.

Malaina rolled her head back and forth trying to sooth her aching neck. "I hope somebody finds us soon," she said to him. Jackson's grin broadened.

"On second thought," Malaina corrected herself, "if anybody found us they'd think..." Malaina's eyes widened and Jackson chuckled. "Jackson! Oh, no! What will folks think?" He opened his eyes to look at her and the look on her face caused him to break into laughter. "It's not funny! This is completely sinful!" she cried.

He erupted into more laughter. "Darlin'...this is survival. We ain't done nothin'. Folks 'round here know that. I guarantee you nobody, but nobody's out lookin' for us in this storm." He lay down again and continued to laugh.

She couldn't help but smile at her own comments. "You're right. People out here are different. They don't just assume the worst."

Jackson sighed as his laughter subsided. "How are you feeling?" he asked.

"Better," she said, reaching back and rubbing her neck. "Just stiff from lying on the ground. How's your shoulder?"

"It don't hurt much. Baker got arrowed once right in the hiney," he chuckled. "Poor boy couldn't sit down for a month. Mama had a crazy fit, of course. We just won't tell her about this. I bet she's worried sick about you," he said frowning.

"She won't worry. She knows I'm with you," Malaina said confidently.

He chuckled again. "That won't give her no comfort necessarily." He winked at her and she blushed. Then a frown crossed his brow again. "She might not even know you're with me. Don't know as anyone saw me get you back there." Jackson began searching the cave. "I need somethin' to hold up these britches."

Malaina stood and went to her drying clothes. "I have a pin in my petticoat that might work." She fumbled around and found it. "Stand up," she said and he did. He hiked up the long johns and held his hand out for the pin. "No, no, no. You hold them like that and...I'll...just...there. See! Now you don't have to worry about..." Her voice gave out as she felt his eyes boring into the top of her head. She slowly looked up at him.

Jackson's jaw was visibly clenched and his chest rose and fell heavily. "I think you better go back to sleep," he mumbled. Malaina noticed how his eyes left her face for a moment and traveled the length of her body and back again.

She giggled nervously. "I must look a sight! Red men's underwear, trap door and all. Look at my hair! All unpinned and wild." She dared to look up at him again.

"You ain't helpin' me out any, Malaina." She cleared her throat and looked away.

"And look at you! Half dressed...as usual...

wounded...pants half falling off." She looked up to find his eyes still burning into hers.

"Go back to sleep, Malaina. Please," he mumbled not moving. Malaina studied Jackson's flawlessly chiseled torso, square clenched jaw, soft tense lips and boyishly tousled hair.

"I don't want to," she whispered as she took a step toward him.

He closed his eyes tightly and frowning shook his head. "Please, sugar. Go over there and go back to sleep for a while."

It must be the fever, for Malaina knew that had she been in her right mind, she would never have taken another step. But she did. She stood so close to him that she could feel the heat from his body.

She gazed up into his brutally handsome face and said, "Bet you a nickel that I can kiss you without touching you, Jackson McCall."

He raised his eyebrows and grinned. "Really?" Malaina smiled and nodded. "All right then. I ain't known as a bettin' man...but I'll call your bluff."

She reached up, taking his whiskery face in her hands and pulled it toward her own. "Do you have a nickel?" she whispered smiling.

"I'm good for it," he said.

Then she touched his lips very softly with hers and the thrill of it caused her to tremble. Malaina stepped back to look at him. He looked just the slightest bit dizzy. She reached into the pocket of her long johns and pulled out the nickel that she'd discovered earlier.

"I guess I should stay away from gambling," she whispered flipping the nickel into the air.

Jackson caught the coin and dropped it in his own pocket. Then he slowly took her into his arms and kissed her forehead.

"Don't go playin' with fire, Miss Malaina. It's mighty unpredictable," he whispered and she thought he would push her away.

But moments later Jackson had made his decision and Malaina felt his coveted kiss on her forehead. Jackson bent and kissed one of her shoulders. Malaina couldn't halt the excitement that flooded her being. When his lips next found her neck, she tightened her grip on his arms, solid as granite. Jackson caressed her neck several times with his kisses and then, as his mouth savored hers, Malaina let her arms slide around his waist, pulling herself tighter to him. His kisses were deep and filled with desire and passion and she returned them with equally as much emotion. She caressed his back, reveling in the feel of the muscles hardening as he worked to hold her tighter. She ran her fingers through his hair, felt his unshaven face, gasped once when he nearly crushed her ribs with his strong hands.

Time was lost to them, until he finally tore his lips from hers and held her to him. His breathing steadied a little. Then he suddenly put her away from him and walked to where their clothes lay by the fire.

"We gotta get home, Malaina," he mumbled. She watched as he angrily pulled on his pants.

Malaina stood stunned and then embarrassed. "I'm

sorry," she said as she reached for her clothing. "What you must think of me." She felt hot tears forming in her eyes.

Jackson grabbed her arm and spun her to face him. "What I think is that you are the only thing in my entire life that I have trouble resistin'! I don't go drinkin'... no gamblin'...no womanizin'...then I find you out in the middle of nowhere and all my self-control goes right out the window. And if I don't get you home, Malaina...I'm gonna end up havin' to make an honest woman of you when I do." Her mouth dropped open in astonishment. "Now...get your clothes on. I'm pretty sure that the storm is over."

CHAPTER THIRTEEN

Jackson and Malaina entered the ranch house kitchen together, finding Mary and Maggie seated at the table, sobbing. Both women looked up with astounded expressions as the tattered couple approached.

"Hi, Mama," Jackson said matter-of-factly as he reached for an apple that sat with several others in a basket on the table.

Malaina didn't utter a word, but flung herself into the parlor and in front of the warm fire. It had been a mere mile, and half another, home. But walking through two feet of snow with no extra clothing for warmth had put her back to the brink of freezing.

Maggie slowly stood, still staring at her son as he followed Malaina to the fire. "Hi, Mama?" she screeched. "Hi, Mama?"

Mary knelt beside Malaina, brushed the tangled hair from her face, studying her features with unspoken awe.

Maggie continued in an emotional voice, "We have been worried near to death, Jackson McCall! The entire town is out searching for you! And for Black Wolf!"

"Oh? Well, they can stop lookin' for him. I killed that dirty son of...I put him out of his misery. And me and Malaina weathered the storm just fine and are home safe and sound," Jackson said as if he'd been out milking the cow all night and day.

Malaina saw the fury rising in Maggie's face.

"Oh. Fine. You killed him," Maggie cried, shaking her head. "We thought you were dead!" Her voice returned to the frightened state as before. "And you waltz in here with a 'Hi, Mama' and grab an apple like you've been out sparkin' after the dance."

Jackson stood and gathered his mother into his arms as she began sobbing. "I'm sorry, Mama. But we really are fine and now we don't have to worry about Black Wolf anymore. We're nearly frozen to the bone, though...and too awful tired to have any emotions left in us. You get Malaina warmed up now and I'll go find the search party and tell 'em we're home."

Malaina watched as the grief stricken mother clung to her baby. "I'll go tell Matthew, Jackson. He's home. He can ride out after them," Mary said, throwing on her coat and heading out the door.

Maggie held her son's face in her hands and smiled up at him through her tears. "You boys scare the life out of me!" Then she looked over at Malaina. Her mouth dropped open as she drew in a horrified breath and moved to her side. The tears began to flow again as she hugged her over and over and wiped her face with her well-worn apron.

"Oh, my baby girl!" she soothed.

"I'm sorry for all the trouble, Mrs. McCall," Malaina forced out in a whisper before bursting into tears of her own and throwing herself into the woman's welcome embrace. Malaina sobbed hard as the older woman consoled her with hushes and kisses on her head, rocking her where they sat on the floor. "I've brought so much trouble on all of you," she cried. "I'm so deeply ashamed of it."

Maggie pushed her back and cupped Malaina's chin firmly in hand, forcing the young woman to look at her. "That is enough, young lady!" she said. "I won't be havin' that kind of talk 'cause it just isn't so. Do you hear me? We wouldn't have life without you now...no we wouldn't. You're our own! Our very own. Do you understand me?"

Malaina nodded only to please the lovely woman. Maggie pulled Malaina to her again. "Now, let's get a tub filled for the two of you, and get somethin' warm down."

Jackson chuckled from his resting place on the sofa. "I think it would be wise to run us each a separate tub, Mama." He grinned and winked at the two women.

Maggie let out a sigh of exasperation. "Well, at least I know now that he's truly unharmed."

Maggie left the room to prepare baths and Malaina stood in front of the fire for several more moments until her teeth quit chattering. At long last she turned to see Jackson asleep on the sofa.

"Jackson?" she whispered. "Jackson? Are you asleep?" No answer and steady breathing indicated that he was.

She crept slowly over until she stood looking down at him. He didn't move.

Malaina knelt and put a hand softly on his knee. "Jackson?" she said again. "Thank you," she whispered as tears brimmed in her eyes once more. "Thank you... for my life...again."

As she stood and turned away Jackson's hand caught her own, startling her. She turned to look at him and watched as he slowly stood up. It was apparent that every muscle and bone in his body pained him. He smiled down at her and she smiled back as she surveyed the tousled hair and dirt smeared face. He looked so boyish.

"I'll tell you what, Little Miss Red Flannel Underwear..." She couldn't stop the blush. He held up one hand and bent one finger at a time down as he spoke. "Let's see, finding you in the desert, pullin' a scorpion outta your drawers, gettin' shot by some varmint who wanted to drag you off from town, killin' an Indian who wanted you...took an arrow by-the-way...and keepin' you from freezin' to death durin' a blizzard." Her spirits began to fall again, but he went on. "I count at least five times that I've saved your dainty little hide. Tell you what..." He looked around sneakily and lowered his voice to a whisper. "You give me one more kiss like you did last night in that cave...and we'll call it even." He grinned down at her surprised face for a moment. Then his smile faded and his brow puckered in a frown. "I won't ever ask again. And life has to return to just the everyday like before, you hear me?" It was a command and she felt her heart sink into the pit of her stomach. "It was all too romantic last night...stuck in the cold with a dusty ol' rancher. I know you weren't in your right mind and I wasn't neither." Malaina's eyebrows lifted at his use of the word 'romantic.' "But, I am a man, after all... and you look mighty cute in red flannels. So, I want a proper 'Thank you, Mr. McCall.'" He grinned at her again, but she felt like running.

In other words, it would have made no difference if the ugliest woman in the world had been in that cave with him. It offended and hurt her. She thought they had shared a loving passion for only each other for a few blissful hours. Now, she knew differently.

Malaina struggled to push herself away from him but he held her tightly. "Take it like I mean it, Malaina... not how it sounded," he said frowning, and she stopped struggling as she felt his lips on her forehead.

A warmth of desire passed through her as his mouth moved to her neck. She let her arms return his embrace and delighted at the feel of him against her. "I saved you for my ownself, you know," he whispered just before he took her mouth roughly with his. The passion was even stronger than before. His kisses were almost uncomfortable at times with their forcefulness and desire.

Jackson tried seven times to end their kisses. It took him eight before his self-control was finally in check. He held her head tightly against his chest once more before breaking the embrace and when he did, he smiled as he ran his thumb over her lips.

"If there were ever gonna be a next time for this...
which there won't...I had better cut off my whiskers
first. I done a job on that petal soft skin of yours." The
skin around her mouth did feel damaged. His whisker
growth was very heavy. "I'm gonna see if Bill made
it home." And he turned and staggered out the front
door.

Malaina stood deeply depressed for several
moments. She hadn't seen Maggie peeking around the
corner at them with a smile as broad as the Mississippi
across her face.

"Come on back, Malaina. Let's get you warmed up,"
Maggie called innocently.

CHAPTER FOURTEEN

Winter came and went without incident. Malaina found that Jackson was true to his word. He had seemingly forgotten her for anything but, perhaps, a sister now. Matthew and Mary had become a charming little couple and Malaina, being Mary's confidant, knew that an engagement would soon be announced and was joyous about it. Baker was still comfortable in his solitude. Malaina wondered if he would simply forever mourn his long lost sweetheart. Maggie was cheerful and smiling all the time and Malaina would often catch her looking lovingly and a bit slyly at her.

"What?" Malaina would ask on such occasions.

"Oh nothin', dear. Nothin' at all," Maggie would chuckle.

Jackson was Jackson. Teasing most of the time, brooding some of the time, and grumpy once in a while. He never seemed to look twice at Malaina, whose dreams continued to be filled with him.

It had been six months since Black Wolf had tried to steal Malaina. She had remembered very little else of her life before she had been found by Jackson and had settled down into family life.

She still broke out in goose bumps whenever Jackson's hand would accidentally brush her in passing, but she knew that he had no interest in her other than as a friend. Probably regarded her as less a chum than he did ol' Bill. Sometimes at night the tears of hurt and aching to be in his arms again would flow steadily·for an hour or so, but she made it through each time.

One morning in early May, Malaina was in the kitchen with a basket of strawberries to be made into jam. She was shamelessly spying on Matthew and Mary who were out by the north fence wrapped in a loving embrace. A grin spread across her face as she peered out the kitchen window and snipped strawberry stems.

"Didn't know you was a 'peepin' tom,' sweetheart." She jumped guiltily as Jackson chuckled behind her.

"Hush!" she shushed him giggling. "They're so cute," she said, smiling and returning to her spying.

He came and stood beside her, peering out the window. "They oughta be...after all your matchmakin' efforts," he chuckled, and her smile faded when he gave her a quick kiss on the cheek as he stole a strawberry.

She turned around to set a bowl of stemmed berries on the table and noticed that blood was saturating a place on the thigh of his pants.

"Is that yours?" she asked irritatedly.

"What?" he asked in return.

"The blood on your pants. Is that yours?" She stood with her hands on her hips in a very scolding and rather maternal manner.

"Well, of course it's mine. You ain't been in any

trouble lately," he said, starting out the door.

Malaina stepped in front of him to stop his escape. "Well, drop 'em and let's get it cleaned up before your mama gets back from the berry patch. She'll tan your hide if you've hurt yourself breaking another horse."

In the previous months Malaina had developed a cast iron stomach when it came to injuries, blood and wounds. The McCall boys were covered in cuts and bruises more often than not.

"Forget about it, Malaina. It's a scratch," he said, trying to move past her.

"Jackson! It'll get infected. You probably cut it on something rusty as well." She innocently reached forward and unfastened his pants.

"Wait a minute! You ain't my mama!" he said, pushing her away.

"Now, Jackson," she ordered. "Do you want me to handle this one, or would you rather bear your mama's wrath about it?"

After considering the question for a split second, Jackson stepped out of his pants, backed up and planted himself on the table.

"Eeewww!" Malaina whined with a grimace as she inspected the wound through the tear in his flannels. "How did you do this one?" she asked as she saturated a cloth in the water that was boiling jam jars on the stove.

"I'm breakin' that new stallion we got. He's purty mean, that one. He threw me and I caught it on a broken fence post...which wouldn't even have been there if Matthew weren't so dang busy sparkin' Mary all the time."

Malaina giggled. "Oh, you're just jealous 'cause he's smooching with a girl and you're out smooching with another horse."

"I ain't jealous, Malaina. Besides, he can't even do a proper job of it. I need to teach that boy a thing or two yet."

Malaina rinsed the blood out of the cloth into the sink and wet it again. "Ha! Quit patting yourself on the back! He's a wonderful, sensitive man. And besides, I've seen them a lot more stuck together than that. It's just daytime and out in the open that's all. I think it's wonderful." She inspected the wound again. "Hmmm. A splinter I think." She used her fingernails to pull it out.

"Whatever happened to that gentle touch you used to have?" he asked.

"Don't be a baby. I swear! You get shot by arrows and bullets and it's no big deal...then you go on and on, whining about a little sticker."

"Well, now this is cute!" Baker chuckled, coming through the back door. "You better hurry up, Malaina. Mama's done pickin'."

Malaina quickly bandaged the wound. But not quickly enough. Maggie stepped through the back door in time to see Jackson pulling up his pants.

"Ah ha! Caught you with your pants down, I see," she laughed as the three guilty faces turned on her. "How bad is it, son?"

"It's just a scratch," Jackson said. "Mama, teach this girl some manners," he said, pointing to Malaina. "She's been spyin' on Matthew and Mary again."

Maggie chuckled and Malaina stuck her tongue out at him in a childish gesture. "Well, maybe she just needs some sparkin' of her own! What do you think?" Maggie teased and didn't miss the look that quickly passed between Jackson and Malaina.

"Well, I oughta be the one to take care of that," Baker said, gathering Malaina into his arms. "What do you say, darlin'? Give us a kiss," he teased, puckering up his lips and trying to kiss her as she giggled and moved her head away.

"Now stop that Baker. We've got berries to do up," Maggie said. She had noticed that Jackson's smile retreated immediately the minute Baker had touched Malaina. She saw his chest rising and falling with heavy breaths even now.

"No more cuts today, Jackson. My stomach can only tolerate one a day," Malaina said as she returned to the berries.

But Jackson simply turned and left the house, slamming the door behind him. Malaina didn't see Baker wink at his mother who winked in return.

❧

Maggie and Malaina put up strawberry preserves and jam for the rest of the morning. Mary helped and they all talked about wedding type things.

"Oh Mary! I can't wait! It's been so long since I've

been to a wedding," Malaina sighed.

"He hasn't officially asked me yet, Malaina. Maybe he won't," Mary said frowning.

"Of course he will," Maggie assured.

It was suppertime when Jackson opened the kitchen door, stepped in and stood looking at them like the grim reaper.

"What is it, boy?" Maggie asked, drying her hands on her apron.

"There's a man in town. Collin Mereaux. From Louisiana," he said.

Malaina dropped the jar of jam she had been holding and put her hands over her mouth. She began walking backwards, shaking her head and muttering, "No! Please! No!" She cried out and her hands pressed against her temples as an excruciating headache began to pound in her brain. The others watched as she crumpled to the floor, sobbing.

"Who is he, Malaina?" Jackson asked in an angry, commanding voice. "I asked you a question!" he yelled.

"Jackson!" Maggie scolded. "Just wait!" She went to where Malaina now lay on the floor crying. "Honey, what is it?" she asked in a soothing voice. "You've got to tell us what you remember."

But the memories were flooding back so painfully and so fast that it was several minutes before she could speak. When she did, she sat up and spoke directly to Jackson. "He owns me," she squeaked out.

"What are you talking about?" Jackson growled angrily.

The memories of her previous life in Louisiana and how she came to be out in the middle of the wilderness were restored to Malaina's conscious. Horrifyingly restored!

"He owns me. I mean...my stepfather sold me to him when my mother died last June. He gave my stepfather an old plantation that he owned and my stepfather turned me over to him in exchange. I don't even know if he intended to marry me...but I was to be his to do with as he would."

Baker and Matthew had since entered the room and everyone stood stunned.

"You mean you're a..." Matthew started, but he broke off as he saw defiance cross her face.

Malaina stood up and slowly walked over to him. "If it were anyone but you, Matthew, I'd slap your face for asking that," she said, holding her head up and trying to stop the tears of hurt. She looked around the room at everyone staring at her. "Is that what you all think of me?" she cried and began to shake.

"No, sweet thing. Of course not!" Maggie said, raising a hand to brush her cheek. Malaina stepped back and out of her reach.

"You do! All of you! You think I'm a...it's not true! I ran away! I would rather have died than...you don't understand! They still fight the war down there! They still think anyone can be sold for the right price!" She felt as if she would vomit. "He even has a so-called legal paper to prove it. He owns me and I ran away."

Everyone in the room was silent for a few moments

and Malaina looked from one to the other.

"Nobody owns anybody, Malaina," Baker said at last.

She giggled nervously. "Maybe not here. But there they do."

"Nowhere, Malaina. Not in the United States," Matthew added.

Malaina felt as if she might faint. It was hard to breath. Baker stepped forward to offer her support.

"Don't touch me!" She looked at Matthew. "How could you believe I could be capable of such a life style?" Mary and Maggie were in tears and Jackson stood staring at her.

"I didn't mean what you thought, Malaina. I wasn't suggestin' that you worked in a...in a...brothel or nothin' like that. I thought maybe you had slave ancestry and that's why he was huntin' you down."

Jackson stood stiff and angry. "She's from the South. Either way it's an insult, little brother," he growled.

"That's not true!" she cried. "I don't feel that way. I've no slave ancestry...but if I did, I wouldn't be ashamed of it." Baker reached for her again.

"Don't!" she cried. Mary burst into sobbing.

Maggie talked quietly. "Malaina, we love you! You're ours. We're you're family! Please, let us help you."

Malaina shook her head furiously. "No. He'll kill you. All of you. He's an evil, evil man." She began looking around frantically. "I'll have to leave! Right now." Then her eyes locked on Jackson. "Please, Jackson. Lend me some money. Help me get away where he won't find me. I beg you."

He looked down into her frightened, pleading face. Then he quickly grabbed her and held her tightly as she struggled.

"Mama, keep her here. I don't care if you have to tie her up! Do you hear me?" Maggie nodded obediently. "Baker, run on out to the barn and saddle up a horse. I want you to ride back to town with me. Matthew... go over to Preacher Pete's house, tell him that if anyone asks...well, he's to say he married me and Malaina last month in private. Get goin'! Keep her here, Mama." And Jackson thrust Malaina into his mother's arms as he started out the door.

"No! Jackson! Don't go! He'll kill you! Please!" Malaina begged through her river of tears.

"Nobody kills me, Malaina. Especially when you're concerned. Calm her down, Mama. She's half outta her mind." And he left.

"Mrs. McCall! You have to stop him! You don't know Collin. Please," the girl begged, slipping to the floor in a near faint. She was unconscious for only a few moments and was a little more rational when she came to.

"There now, sweet pea. You're fine and everythin' will work out," Maggie cooed.

"Mrs. McCall, please...you don't know this man," Malaina pleaded. "Jackson is overconfident...to say the least. He'll be killed!"

Maggie spoke sharply. "Get control of yourself,

Malaina. First of all, in this family...everybody's problems concern everybody. Second...Jackson talks a big game because he's capable of it. Don't you know that by now?"

Malaina nodded. She did know it. She had no doubt that face-to-face Collin was no threat to Jackson. But Collin Mereaux was an evil, vile, corrupt, and yet spineless man who always traveled with his personal thugs. She worried, for Jackson could well find himself facing ten men to his one.

Maggie went on, "We'll wait here. The boys will take care of this."

So, they waited. The three women sat together in ominous silence as the minutes passed. The clock on the mantel numbered those long, tedious mintues and eventually struck the hour. Malaina closed her beautiful eyes in unspoken prayer as the clock marked yet another hour.

And then, as if the clock's striking was to summon a dreadful premonition, their hearts leapt at the sound of approaching riders.

Malaina sprinted out the door. "Jackson! What's going on?" There was no answer and her lovely hands gripped the porch railing tightly for support as she saw before her the heinous Collin Mereaux mounted on a violent black stallion kicking at the dirt and snorting angrily as his master reined him to a halt. "Collin," she gasped, feeling as if someone had drained the lifeblood from her.

How could she have possibly forgotten this man?

He was tall, not unusually handsome like Jackson, but considered very handsome just the same. Black hair, black eyes, white teeth and wicked smile. And now he was before her with at least four other men behind him.

"Yes, darling. So, you've regained your precious memory. We had been informed that it was lost for some time," he said mockingly.

As his repulsively familiar voice echoed in her brain she ordered, "Go away, Collin," and hoped the fear in her intonation wasn't too apparent.

"Oh, but, I've come to rescue you, my beauty." He dismounted and Malaina resisted the urge to step back.

"I'm afraid you'll have to leave, sir. You're not welcome here," Maggie said, stepping through the door to stand next to Malaina.

Collin laughed. "Well, I'm certain that is an understatement, ma'am."

As Malaina looked then to Maggie, complete and absolute understanding sparked within her bosom. Maggie loved her! She loved her as she would her own daughter. A moment before she had appeared at her side, Malaina had contemplated conceding defeat to Collin, thereby preserving each precious life in the McCall family. But now she knew that she could never endure such an existence. Death would be more tolerable an anticipation. She further knew that if she were to be taken by him, the pain inflicted upon this uniquely brave and beautiful woman would be too cruelly administered. Baker and Matthew were both willing to protect her with their lives as they would, no doubt, their own sister, had they been blessed with one. And Jackson...yes, Jackson. Jackson had proven time and again that he would forfeit his own life to preserve hers. She thought of him now, her champion, her dream lover. She could not leave him. Better to perish and pass to the next life than to leave him, knowing she would have to endure the touch of another man.

"We're not alone here, Collin," Malaina stated bravely.

"Hmmm. Yes. So I hear," he mumbled, moving closer to them.

Malaina still stood her ground. The severe shock that the horrible memories rushing back had left was gone and she was herself, in control again. Barely. He approached until he stood directly before her. Then he reached out and touched her cheek. She pulled away, sickened.

"I've been searching for so long, darling. Think how it must be for me...anticipating having such a beauty as you for my own...and then...poof...you're gone." He reached to touch her again. Malaina stepped back out of his reach. "How very rude and quite unbecoming, darling. After all, I've come to take you home," Collin chuckled.

"You know that I won't go with you, Collin. And I've friends now to protect me," Malaina stated flatly, though she felt everything within her quivering with fear. Still she would stand stalwart. Nothing could tear her from her course.

"I would suggest that you leave our property at

once, mister. And for your own well bein'...I wouldn't be tryin' to bother my son's wife again," Maggie added boldly.

Collin sneered and said, "Don't tell me you've gone and married one of these...these...farmers, Malaina?"

Malaina raised her chin proudly as Collin chuckled. Snapping his fingers, he motioned to the men that accompanied him and ordered, "Bring her forward, Jon."

Malaina watched as one of the riders dismounted, dragged another rider from his own mount and forcing him forward. She gasped in astounded horror as Collin proceeded to brutally rip the hat from the smaller rider's head, revealing the hauntingly familiar face.

"Charlotte!" she cried out.

"Yes. Our dearest Charlotte," Collin confirmed.

Charlotte burst into tears and was undoubtedly scared beyond rational behavior. Malaina stared disbelieving at the young woman who bore her similar likeness. Blue eyes, black hair, and beauty. "If you've harmed her, Collin..." Malaina began.

"What, darling? What will you do?" he mocked. "Now, there, there...Charlotte," he muttered to the girl, putting a hand caressively to her face.

"Don't touch her!" Malaina screamed, gripping the railing even more solidly.

As Collin sighed triumphantly, Maggie looked to Malaina for explanation. "Who is she?" she asked.

"My half sister, Charlotte," Malaina mumbled.

"Yes," Collin chuckled. "Dear, dear Charlotte. The

spoiled baby sister. Though you do love her, don't you, Malaina? Charlotte was always good to you. Even though your stepfather sold you to me so that his own daughter could have a dowry. Sad...but true. Now, come along with me, Malaina."

"Malaina don't listen to him! Please!" Charlotte pleaded.

"What do you want of me, Collin?" Malaina asked defeatedly. Charlotte was her sister, and she loved her deeply. There was no other choice.

He smiled. "Why...you of course, my dear. You come with me now...no more running away...and I'll leave dear Charlotte here in your place. Otherwise, I'll kill her here and now before your very eyes."

"Nobody's goin' anywhere, mister."

Malaina turned to see Mary coming out of the house, a rifle raised and pointed at Collin's head. Slowly she went to stand before him as she spoke once more. "You get outta here. Leave the girl, too."

Reaching out quickly, Collin grabbed the gun barrel, tearing the weapon from her grasp. "Come now, miss...don't be silly." Mary gasped and stepped back from him.

"You're a pretty one as well, miss," Collin said, tossing the gun aside. Then in one swift motion he had turned Mary to face the others, staying her with one hand while the other pulled a revolver from beneath his coat and held it to the girl's head.

"Mary!" Maggie cried out.

"Collin...please," Malaina began. "Let her go. Please."

"Now this is comforting, Malaina. Pleading with me...as it were." Collin nuzzled Mary's neck, however, commenting, "She's sweet as magnolia in summer. What do you say, honeysuckle? Perhaps you and I could enjoy a satisfying moment or two before I move on to my dear Malaina there. What do you say?"

"Get your filthy, smelly hands off her!"

Hope was renewed within Malaina as she saw Matthew approaching from one side of the house. He'd obviously returned and seen the trouble they were in. He now leveled his own rifle at the villain's head.

Chuckling, Collin turned to face him still holding Mary in front of him with the pistol pressed firmly to her temple. "Ah. A farm boy. Don't trifle with me, boy...or this little miss won't be of any use to any of you. Except as perhaps fertilizer for your pitiful little crops come next spring. Put the gun away, boy. Or I'll start the job for you with her brains. You could plant a lovely little flower bed just here...where her blood first spills."

Malaina watched as Matthew's chest rose and fell with fiery anger. She watched as an anguished expression crossed his face when he realized that the risk of Collin successfully shooting Mary should he attempt to fell the monster himself was more than he could chance.

Angrily, Matthew tossed his gun aside. "Let her go, then," he ordered.

"Your wish is my command," Collin said. However,

in that next moment, he pushed Mary to the ground, pointed his gun at the young champion and fired. Matthew's hand flew to his head and he staggered forward slightly before falling to the ground.

Mary screamed and Maggie screeched, "Matthew!" as the handsome young man lay silent and motionless a few feet away.

Malaina began shaking her head and muttering to herself, "No. No." As she started toward the fallen hero, Collin kicked Mary squarely in the stomach and grabbed Malaina by the arm, staying her.

Yanking at her mercilessly he pulled her against his powerful body. Looking down at the breathless, heartbroken and battered Mary he said, "No woman threatens me with a weapon, girl. Be glad you have your life." Then he turned to Malaina, still holding her securely. "I own you, Malaina. He's dead now. Forget your dirty little farm boy." Reaching into his inner coat pocket, Collin retrieved a folded document. "My papers, Malaina. A bill of sale signed by your dearly departed stepfather."

Malaina reached up and slapped him hard across the face. He instantly slapped her back, leaving horridly red welts fresh upon her tender cheek.

"Leave her alone, Collin!" Charlotte shouted. "I told you...I'll take her place!"

"I don't want you, Charlotte. I want your sister, and I own her. Legally."

Then the sickening, wet kiss of Collin Mereaux met Malaina's mouth. Her defeated heart cried out for

Jackson--for his powerful arms to be protectively about her. For his mouth to be warm and tenderly passionate upon her own. At last her struggling won out and he released the nauseating seal his lips had on hers.

"Get the other girl back on her horse, men. We're going home," Collin commanded, laughing triumphantly.

Charlotte screamed, "No!" as the men accompanying Collin dismounted. Two of them took hold of Charlotte, dragging her toward a mount as another man assisted Collin in pulling Malaina toward the waiting group of horses.

"You promised, Collin!" Malaina cried, struggling with all the strength left in her. "You promised to leave Charlotte!"

"Did I?" Collin mocked. "Oh, fiddle. We'll bring her along...just in case you decide not to...cooperate fully with me."

"Malaina!" Maggie cried as Mary at last was able to rush to Matthew.

"Leave it be, old mother," Collin warned Maggie. "I would as soon shoot her than take such a large financial loss. Do you know how much I paid for this piece of fluff?"

Malaina watched helplessly as the sister she loved so was lifted onto the horse, her hands then bound to the saddle horn. Collin shoved Malaina onto his own horse, bound her hands as well, and mounted behind her.

"I do thank you, old woman...for keeping her in

good repair for me," Collin said. Then Malaina felt all hope...the very will to live...draining from her as his repulsive lips toyed at her neck. She painfully looked at Matthew's still body and Mary hovering over him sobbing.

It felt suddenly as if some all-powerful force hit Collin solidly, sending him falling from the horse. Her eyes fell to where he lay on the ground and resplendent joy was rekindled as she saw the man being beaten mercilessly by Jackson. Jackson's horse stood snorting and rearing next to the one she sat on. She hadn't heard him approach, yet he was there! Ever her protector.

"You dirty..." Jackson mumbled as his fists dealt blow after blow to the surprised man. He stopped abruptly, however, when three guns were cocked simultaneously, pointing at his head. Collin's men encircled Jackson and Jackson ceased beating Collin and stood.

"Jackson," Malaina squeaked out in a whisper. He looked to her only for a moment before returning his attention to the villain.

Collin stood, brushing himself off dramatically. "This is a silk shirt, sir," he informed Jackson.

"Yeah? Well it figures you'd wear somethin' that came outta a worm's behind," Jackson growled.

Collin cleared his throat and smoothed his hair. "Am I to understand that I've disposed of the wrong... husband?" he asked sarcastically.

"That's my brother lyin' over there," Jackson confirmed. His face blatantly displayed anger, disgust and hatred toward the man who stood before him.

"Even though you killed my brother...I mighta shown some mercy and killed you quick. But you laid your filthy hands on Malaina. And for that I intend to make your death as slow and painful as possible. I ain't never skinned a man before...though, I hear that some Indian tribes find that the most painful way to kill a man. Yer purty much neck deep in bull manure, mister." Malaina had never seen Jackson in such a state of vindictive hatred and rage. She was sure he meant to kill Collin as gruesomely as he had just described.

"Jackson, no, please," Malaina pleaded, "I'll go with him! I don't want you to have to..."

"You'll never go with him, Malaina! Not as long as I have breath in me."

"Which won't be long," Collin sneered. He looked to Malaina. "Don't tell me you actually married this... illiterate trash? Oh, Malaina, Malaina, Malaina. You know that you're mine. Your marriage changes nothing." He pulled the document from his vest pocket once more, flaunting it in Jackson's face. "My papers, um...sir. I own this girl. I've just come to collect the property that is mine, by law," he said.

Jackson smiled, snatched the papers from his hand and said, "I know some of you folks have a hard time accepting this, but the war is over...the North won and Lincoln freed the slaves. No court is gonna hold to anythin' so asinine as papers that say you own a woman."

"She's my property," Collin said as his smile faded.

"Nope. It just ain't so. You see...every court in this

good country would most certainly hold to the paper *I* have concernin' this woman," Jackson said.

Collin looked about him, motioning to the men who held Jackson at gunpoint. "Well, no court's going to enter into it, farmer. Either you're blind or else you're too ignorant to realize that you are at a severe disadvantage. The South will, indeed, triumph this time. Let's just shoot him and get on with our journey, boys."

"I'm really very surprised and disappointed, sir," Jackson addressed Collin. "I always thought you Southern boys were so brave and chivalrous. I never thought you'd be hidin' behind hired guns. I heard you boys always fought your own duels. But, then, I guess you'd be havin' to get that wormy ol' shirt all mussed up again. Is that it?"

Malaina looked at Jackson in dismay. She knew he'd struck at the pride in the enemy. A dangerous attack, for Collin was nothing if not prideful.

The rage of the insult shown clearly on Collin's face. "Do not toy with me, farmer. I'll easily dispose of you."

Jackson grinned. "Now, by law, Malaina here is my wife...you can't take her. But, since you're such a lily soft boy, I'll let you pick the way I kill you. Gun, fists, or..."

"Sabers," Collin stated without hesitation. Motioning to his men to lower their guns, he took several steps toward Jackson.

"Sabers?" Jackson repeated.

"What's wrong? You said I could choose, you swine."

Jackson nodded. Malaina turned to Maggie who had exhaled an audible sigh of triumph. Collin seemed to ignore her, while Malaina wondered if the strain had been too much on her mind, for she appeared to be somehow relieved slightly.

Straightening his vest, Collin said, "Very well. I assume you'll be needing a saber. I've several with me." He turned. But Jackson's next utterance stopped him.

"Nope. Got my very own right upstairs. I'll have my mama fetch it." Then, turning to his mother he instructed, "Mama, would you run along up to my trunk and get my saber?" He tossed a key to her as the fear began to intensify in Malaina again.

"So," Collin began, "you've a little trinket from the war or some such thing."

"Nope. It's my own. To do a little pattin' my ownself on the back, I was best man with a saber for every one of my four years at West Point."

Malaina looked at Jackson in astonishment. Black Wolf slipped into her thoughts as she now understood why the beast had referred to Jackson as 'Captain.'

Jackson grinned at Collin. "You see, sir...I'm not what you thought you'd run into out here...am I?"

But Collin was all too confident. "What a nice bit of exercise this will be. Should last all of three minutes."

"You think that long?" Jackson asked mockingly.

"It depends on how fast the blood will drain from that sun roasted body of yours, boy."

"A lot slower than it will from your lily-white

hide. Remember, I ain't the one who has to buy me a woman," Jackson chuckled.

Maggie returned then, and handed a beautiful saber to Jackson. She glared at Collin, reassured in her knowledge of her son's skill and said, "Well, Mr. Collin whoever you are...you're a mighty brave man if'n you think you can go saber to saber with Captain Jackson McCall and come out standin'."

"Is that so?" Collin mocked.

Malaina screamed as Collin took a swipe at Jackson with his saber, cutting him deeply on one arm.

"Just a little taste of the mutilation you're about to endure, farmer," Collin chuckled.

Jackson retaliated then, cutting Collin nicely across one cheek in response. "All right, you purty little pansy...come on. I'm gonna carve you up with the McCall brand before I finish you, you coward."

Malaina was unable to tear her eyes from the nightmare that was the duel. She found herself holding her breath every time Collin lunged toward Jackson, and releasing it in relief as he parried and returned blows of his own. Oddly fascinated, she watched as Jackson's saber met again with Collin's cheek, the two wounds now forming what appeared to be an inverted V. Jackson lunged forward several times in sequence, forcing Collin backward, away from Maggie, Mary and Matthew. Collin was startled as Jackson masterfully inflicted the wounded cheek with two more small lacerations, completing a perfect letter 'M' there. The villain was stunned and raised his free hand to the wound. His face registered fear and shock as he pulled the hand away and saw his own blood forming an 'M' in the palm of his hand. Malaina watched the beads of perspiration dripping from Collin's brow and triumph rose within her when Jackson completed the McCall brand by adding a bar above the letter with one final stroke.

Her joyous elation was short lived, however, as Collin, realizing that he was out-matched by the 'farmer,' barked a final order to his men. "Shoot the Captain!"

"No!" Malaina screamed. Shots rang out in that moment and she was utterly confused as she saw two of Collin's men fall to the ground.

"Move away from my brother, boys." Baker appeared from the opposite side of the house. In his hands he held a rifle aimed squarely at Collin's head.

"Shoot him!" Collin shouted to his last standing man. Instantly Jackson lunged forward, fatally wounding the remaining man with the saber he still held.

The horses that Malaina and Charlotte sat tied to began to rear, spooked by the gunfire. Malaina saw Baker grab Charlotte's horse by the bit, controlling the startled mare. Jackson turned from Collin and tried to grab the reins of Malaina's panicked mount. They eluded his grasp, however, and Malaina gasped in horror as Collin grasped his saber firmly with both hands and raised it above his head clearly intent on ramming it through Jackson's back. Another shot rang out then, and Collin fell to the ground.

"Matthew!" Malaina heard Maggie cry just as her horse bolted away.

As the horse ran from the ranch at a fierce gallop, she could feel the saddle slipping. She found it utterly impossible to gain control of the horse or regain her own balance with her hands tied as they were. But, as always, Jackson was soon at her side on his own mount. He whistled and shouted and the horse reared, stomping his hooves, and turned back toward the ranch, slowing its pace in the process. Malaina could see the house again--beacon of safety and love. Maggie and Mary were helping Matthew to his feet. Baker was holding Charlotte protectively in his arms. Malaina was feeling the warmth of security beginning to ebb through her when the horse lost its footing. She heard the snap of leather and felt the sensation of falling. Then her soul memorized the looks of horror on the faces of the family as she plummeted toward the ground.

"Malaina!" Jackson's anguished voice called. Her last thoughts before the terrible weight and darkness were, 'He's alive. My Jackson is alive.'

❧

"She's breathing." The voices sounded distant and distorted.

"Pull him up! We've got to get him off!" It was Jackson's voice and there was something frantic about it.

Malaina tried to open her eyes. She tried to force her throat to speak, but nothing would come. She was aware then of a great weight being lifted from her legs.

168

"He's up! He's up!" Baker shouted.

"Malaina? Malaina? Please...open them beautiful eyes and look at me, darlin'," Jackson's voice echoed in her mind. "Baker, get her hands free from the horn. Come on, honey. Look at me. You know you want to. Ain't too many ol' boys 'round here that can beat me in good looks. You know that," he said. "Baker," he shouted, "get these dang ropes cut, will you. Mama, her wrists are bleedin' somethin' awful." His intonation was harsh and unstable.

"I'm workin' as fast as I can, Jack," Baker assured him.

The stinging pain in her wrists as the ropes came free caused Malaina to gasp, filling her lungs with life giving air. Still she could not speak.

"Dang!" she heard Jackson mutter under his breath, and she felt herself being pulled into his urgent embrace. "Don't you dare leave me, darlin'!" His calloused, gentle hands tenderly stroked her hair. Though she longed to gaze into his soft green eyes, to speak, reassuring him that she would be fine, her body refused to respond.

"Malaina. It's Maggie." Maggie's voice was so soothing. "I'm wrappin' those little hands of yours in my apron, sweet pea." Malaina sensed the pressure of Maggie's hands on her throbbing wrists. "Charlotte is safe with Baker, Malaina. Everything is fine now. Matthew was only grazed in the head." Maggie's concern and fatigued emotions were evident in the cracking of her voice as she continued, "Mary's fine, too, and you're gonna be fine. Do you hear?"

"Please, Malaina," Jackson's voice pleaded. Malaina could feel the warmth of his breath on her cheek. She smelled the familiar aroma of leather and bacon that was his. "I can't lose you now, darlin'. Do you think I saved your hide time after time to let you go now? I even had the white horse this time, Malaina."

"White horse?" she heard herself whisper.

She was aware of Jackson sighing heavily and hugging her tightly against him. As her eyes at last opened they beheld the magnificent face of her champion.

"You said yourself, way back when, that all I needed was a white horse," he said, smiling and kissing her cheek softly as he stroked her hair affectionately.

As she gazed into his handsome face and her mind became clearer, she realized fully the danger they had all just endured. She was angry with herself for subjecting them all to such peril. Especially Jackson. She looked at the blood dried on his sleeve. The blood from the wound inflicted because of her.

Pushing him away she cried, "How dare you? Sabers! Of all things! Why did you have to make it into such a game? It was awful! He could've killed you!" she buried her face in her hands, sobbing violently with emotional relief.

Taking her gently by the shoulders, Jackson again drew her to him. "Sshh, darlin'. It's all over," he whispered into her hair.

Malaina let her arms slip around him, hugging him tightly against her own body. "He could've killed you, Jackson," she reminded.

"He didn't, Malaina," he reminded in return. Then he chuckled, "He couldn't a won anyway. I didn't spend no four years at West Point to get whipped by some man who wears ruffles on his chest."

"It's not funny. How can you laugh? I thought I'd have to see you be killed!" she cried, hugging him tighter.

His smile showed compassion, not mockery. "I know, darlin'. But it's over now. No more worries. No more strangers showin' up to try and steal you away." He kissed her cheek tenderly and began playing with a lock of her soft hair. His eyes hypnotized her as he spoke. "Now, I figure...I've saved you again, right?" He kissed her other cheek. "That's six times now, ain't it?" He kissed her forehead. "I figure...you marry me and we'll call it even."

"But you said..." she began. Her words were silenced and her eyes widened in disbelief as he pressed a lovingly passionate kiss to her mouth.

"I was afraid, Malaina," he confessed and his smile was gone. "Afraid that you'd suddenly remember someday...someone in the past that you loved before. Someone you'd regret losing. Someone that you'd come to realize you loved more than your smelly ol' cowboy." Tears rolled from Malaina's eyes and down her temples and she tried to smile.

"But, I own you now. And I've got the papers to prove it." He kissed her quickly again, waved Collin's 'legal' bill of sale in her face, stuffed it in his shirt and smiled as she pulled his head to hers to return his kisses.

Maggie and Mary were wiping their tears of joy with their strawberry and blood stained aprons. "A double wedding!" Maggie sighed.

"Malaina!" Charlotte exclaimed in horror as she watched her sister receiving and returning passionate kisses with Jackson. "Malaina! How can you? It's so improper! Such intimate behavior. In public! Not to mention kneeling in the soil...with a man!" Malaina laughed as she looked up at her sister's blushing face.

Jackson chuckled and winked at Baker. "I saw you lookin' at that girl, Baker. Take off your shirt and start breakin' her in!"

Baker grinned and turned to Charlotte. She was quite beautiful herself. He'd felt something toward her instantly. She clutched her shirt collar.

"Baker!" Maggie warned. But he ignored her.

"Ma'am," he said, taking Charlotte in his arms and forcing his proficient kiss on her mouth. She struggled at first but then relented and returned his kiss for a moment before he released her.

Maggie smiled when she saw the look that passed between Charlotte and her middle son. Yes. She thought. They'd all be married soon.

Happiness for Charlotte caused Malaina's heart to swell to near bursting. For she, too, had seen the undeniable expression of love at first sight that passed between Baker and her beloved sister.

Jackson pulled Malaina to her feet after he'd stood himself. Everyone was going into the house. Mary was chattering to Matthew about tending to his wound, Baker was looking dreamily down at the blushing Miss Charlotte and Maggie was babbling about her new daughter.

"I've loved you from the very first moment, Malaina. I tried and tried to talk myself out of it," Jackson said, pulling her to him.

"Why?" she asked, nuzzling her forehead into his neck.

"I'm a sweaty ol' cowboy who's always beat up and couldn't talk good grammar if my life depended on it. And look at you...all beautiful and soft like a peach in summer. What do you want me for?"

She looked up at him and he played with a strand of her hair in his mouth.

"You smell like heaven," she said smiling. "You're every girl's dream...handsome, strong, intelligent, a survivor, a protector...and I'm sure you're every bit the lover that you make yourself out to be."

"That I am, my darlin'. That I am." And he kissed her again to prove it.

My everlasting admiration, gratitude and love…
To my husband, Kevin…
My inspiration…
My heart's desire…
The man of my every dream!

ABOUT THE AUTHOR

Marcia Lynn McClure's intoxicating succession of novels, novellas, and e-books—including *The Visions of Ransom Lake*, *A Crimson Frost*, *The Rogue Knight*, and most recently *The Pirate Ruse*—has established her as one of the most favored and engaging authors of true romance. Her unprecedented forte in weaving captivating stories of western, medieval, regency, and contemporary amour void of brusque intimacy has earned her the title "The Queen of Kissing."

Marcia, who was born in Albuquerque, New Mexico, has spent her life intrigued with people, history, love, and romance. A wife, mother, grandmother, family historian, poet, and author, Marcia Lynn McClure spins her tales of splendor for the sake of offering respite through the beauty, mirth, and delight of a worthwhile and wonderful story.

Bibliography

(By first *in print* publishing date.)

The Heavenly Surrender (2001, 2002, 2009, 2011)
The Visions of Ransom Lake (2002, 2007)
Shackles of Honor (2002, 2009)
Dusty Britches (2003, 2008)
Desert Fire (2003)
To Echo the Past (2003, 2011)
The Fragrance of her Name (2004, 2009)
An Old-Fashioned Romance (2004, 2010)
Divine Deception (2005)
The Touch of Sage (2007, 2010)
Daydreams (2007)
Born for Thorton's Sake (2007)
Sudden Storms (2007, 2011)
The Whispered Kiss (2008)
The Prairie Prince (2008)
The Highwayman of Tanglewood (2008)
Love Me (2009)
The Time of Aspen Falls (2009)
A Crimson Frost (2009)
Saphyre Snow (2009)
Beneath the Honeysuckle Vine (2009)
Weathered Too Young (2010)
The Windswept Flame (2010)
Romantic Vignettes, The Anthology of Premiere Novellas (2010)
The Pirate Ruse (2010)
The Rogue Knight (2010)
The Heavenly Surrender Limited 10th Anniversary Collector's Edition
(2011)
Kissing Cousins (2011)
The Trove of the Passion Room (2011)
Sweet Cherry Ray (2011)
Midnight Masquerade (2011)
The Light of the Lovers' Moon (2011)
Kiss in the Dark (2011)

The Tide of the Mermaid Tears (2011)
A Better Reason to Fall in Love (2011)
Take a Walk With Me (2011)

To Echo the Past
Historical Romance

As her family abandoned the excitement of the city for the uneventful lifestyle of a small, western town, Brynn Clarkston's worst fears were realized. Stripped of her heart's hopes and dreams, Brynn knew true loneliness.

Until an ordinary day revealed a heavenly oasis in the desert…Michael McCall. Handsome and irresistibly charming, Michael McCall (the son of legendary horse breeder Jackson McCall) seemed to offer wild distraction and sincere friendship to Brynn. But could Brynn be content with mere friendship when her dreams of Michael involved so much more?

The Pirate Ruse
Historical Romance

Abducted! Forcibly taken from her home in New Orleans, Cristabel Albay found herself a prisoner aboard an enemy ship—and soon thereafter, transferred into the vile hands of blood-thirsty pirates! War waged between the newly liberated United States and King George. Still, Cristabel would soon discover that British sailors were the very least of her worries—for the pirate captain, Bully Booth, owned no loyalty—no sympathy for those he captured.

Yet hope was not entirely lost—for where there was found one crew of pirates—there was ever found another. Though Cristabel Albay would never have dreamed that she may find fortune in being captured by one pirate captain only to be taken by another—she did! Bully Booth took no man alive—let no woman live long. But the pirate Navarrone was known for his clemency. Thus, Cristabel's hope in knowing her life's continuance was restored.

Nonetheless, as Cristabel's heart began to yearn for the affections of her handsome, beguiling captor—she wondered if Captain Navarrone had only saved her life to execute her poor heart!

Weathered Too Young
Historical Romance

Lark Lawrence was alone. In all the world there was no one who cared for her. Still, there were worse things than independence—and Lark had grown quite capable of providing for herself. Nevertheless, as winter loomed, she suddenly found herself with no means by which to afford food and shelter—destitute.

Yet Tom Evans was a kind and compassionate man. When Lark Lawrence appeared on his porch, without pause he hired her to keep house and cook for himself and his cantankerous elder brother, Slater. And although Tom had befriend Lark first, it would be Slater Evans—handsome, brooding, and twelve years Lark's senior—who would unknowingly abduct her heart.

Still, Lark's true age (which she concealed at first meeting the Evans brothers) was not the only truth she had kept from Slater and Tom Evans. Darker secrets lay imprisoned deep within her heart—and her past.

However, it is that secrets are made to be found out—and Lark's secrets revealed would soon couple with the arrival of a woman from Slater's past to forever shatter her dreams of winning his love—or so it seemed. Would truth and passion mingle to capture Lark the love she'd never dared to hope for?

The Windswept Flame
Historical Romance

Broken—irreparably broken. The violent deaths of her father and the young man she'd been engaged to marry had irrevocably broken Cedar Dale's heart. Her mother's heart had been broken as well—shattered by the loss of her own true love. Thus, pain and anguish—fear and despair—found Cedar Dale and her mother, Flora, returned to the small western town where life had once been happy and filled with hope. Perhaps there Cedar and her mother would find some resemblance of truly living life—instead of merely existing. And then, a chance meeting with a dream from her past caused a flicker of wonder to ignite in her bosom.

As a child, Cedar Dale had adored the handsome rancher's son, Tom Evans. And when chance brought her face-to-face with the object of her childhood fascination once more, Cedar Dale began to believe that perhaps her fragmented heart could be healed.

Yet could Cedar truly hope to win the regard of such a man above men as was Tom Evans? A man kept occupied with hard work and ambition—a man so desperately sought after by seemingly every woman?

Beneath the Honeysuckle Vine
Historical Romance

Civil War—no one could flee from the nightmare of battle and the countless lives it devoured. Everyone had sacrificed—suffered profound misery and unimaginable loss. Vivianna Bartholomew was no exception. The war had torn her from her home—orphaned her. The merciless war seemed to take everything—even the man she loved. Still, Vivianna yet knew gratitude—for a kind friend had taken her in upon the death of her parents. Thus, she was cared for—even loved.

Yet as General Lee surrendered, signaling the war's imminent end—as Vivianna remained with the remnants of the Turner family—her soul clung to the letters written by her lost soldier—to his memory written in her heart. Could a woman ever heal from the loss of such a love? Could a woman's heart forget that it may find another? Vivianna Bartholomew thought not.

Still, it is often in the world that miracles occur—that love endures even after hope has been abandoned. Thus, one balmy Alabama morning—as two ragged soldiers wound the road toward the Turner house—Vivianna began to know—to know that miracles do exist—that love is never truly lost.

A Crimson Frost
Historical Romance

Beloved of her father, King Dacian, and adored by her people, the Scarlet Princess Monet endeavored to serve her kingdom well—for the people of the Kingdom of Karvana were good and worthy of service. Long Monet had known that even her marriage would serve her people. Her husband would be chosen for her—for this was the way of royal existence.

Still, as any woman does—peasant or princess— Monet dreamt of owning true love—of owning choice in love. Thus, each time the raven-haired, sapphire-eyed, Crimson Knight of Karvana rode near, Monet knew regret—for in secret, she loved him—and she could not choose him.

As an arrogant king from another kingdom began to wage war against Karvana, Karvana's king, knights, and soldiers answered the challenge. The Princess Monet would also know battle. As the Crimson Knight battled with armor and blade—so the Scarlet Princess would battle in sacrifice and with secrets held. Thus, when the charge was given to preserve the heart of Karvana—Monet endeavored to serve her kingdom and forget her secreted love. Yet love is not so easily forgotten…

Saphyre Snow
Historical Romance

Descended of a legendary line of strength and beauty, Saphyre Snow had once known happiness as princess of the Kingdom of Graces. Once a valiant king had ruled in wisdom—once a loving mother had spoken soft words of truth to her daughter. Yet a strange madness had poisoned great minds—a strange fever inviting Lord Death to linger. Soon it was even Lord Death sought to claim Saphyre Snow for his own—and all Saphyre loved seemed lost.

Thus, Saphyre fled—forced to leave all familiars for necessity of preserving her life. Alone, and without provision, Saphyre knew Lord Death might yet claim her—for how could a princess hope to best the Reaper himself?

Still, fate often provides rescue by extraordinary venues, and Saphyre was not delivered into the hands of Death—but into the hands of those hiding dark secrets in the depths of bruised and bloodied souls. Saphyre knew a measure of hope and asylum in the company of these battered vagabonds. Even she knew love—a secreted love—a forbidden love. Yet it was love itself—even held secret—that would again summon Lord Death to hunt the princess, Saphyre Snow.

The Highwayman of Tanglewood
Historical Romance

A chambermaid in the house of Tremeshton, Faris Shayhan well knew torment, despair, and trepidation. To Faris it seemed the future stretched long and desolate before her—bleak and as dark as a lonesome midnight path. Still, the moon oft casts hopeful luminosity to light one's way. So it was that Lady Maranda

Rockrimmon cast hope upon Faris—set Faris upon a different path—a path of happiness, serenity, and love.

Thus, Faris abandoned the tainted air of Tremeshton in favor of the amethyst sunsets of Loch Loland Castle and her new mistress, Lady Rockrimmon. Further, it was on the very night of her emancipation that Faris first met the man of her dreams—the man of every woman's dreams—the rogue Highwayman of Tanglewood.

Dressed in black and astride his mighty steed, the brave, heroic, and dashing rogue Highwayman of Tanglewood stole Faris's heart as easily as he stole her kiss. Yet the Highwayman of Tanglewood was encircled in mystery—mystery as thick and as secretive as time itself. Could Faris truly own the heart of a man so entirely enveloped in twilight shadows and dangerous secrets?

The Visions of Ransom Lake
Historical Romance

Youthful beauty, naïve innocence, a romantic imagination thirsting for adventure…an apt description of Vaden Valmont, who would soon find the adventure and mystery she had always longed to experience…in the form of a man.

A somber recluse, Ransom Lake descended from his solitary concealment in the mountains, wholly uninterested in people and their trivial affairs. And somehow, young Vaden managed to be ever in his way…either by accident or because of her own unique ability to stumble into a quandary.

Yet the enigmatic Ransom Lake would involuntarily become Vaden's unwitting tutor. Through him, she would experience joy and passion the like even Vaden had never imagined. Yes, Vaden Valmont stepped innocently, yet irrevocably, into love with the secretive, seemingly callous man.

But there were other life's lessons Ransom Lake would inadvertently bring to her as well. The darker side of life—despair, guilt, heartache. Would Ransom Lake be the means of Vaden's dreams come true? Or the cause of her complete desolation?

The Touch of Sage
Historical Romance

After the death of her parents, Sage Willows had lovingly nurtured her younger sisters through childhood, seeing each one married and never resenting not finding herself a good man to settle down with. Yet, regret is different than resentment.

Still, Sage found as much joy as a lonely young woman could find, as proprietress of Willows's Boarding House—finding some fulfillment in the companionship of the four beloved widow women boarding with her. But when the devilishly handsome Rebel Lee Mitchell appeared on the boarding house step, Sage's contentment was lost forever.

Dark, mysterious and secretly wounded, Reb Mitchell instantly captured Sage's lonely heart. But the attractive cowboy, admired and coveted by every young unmarried female in his path, seemed unobtainable to Sage Willows. How could a weathered, boarding house proprietress resigned to spinsterhood ever hope to capture the attention of such a man? And without him, would Sage Willows simply sink deeper into bleak loneliness—tormented by the knowledge that the man of every woman's dreams could never be hers?

The Whispered Kiss
Historical Romance

With the sea at its side, the beautiful township of Bostchelan was home to many—including the lovely Coquette de Bellamont, her three sisters, and beloved father. In Bostchelan, Coquette knew happiness and as much contentment as a young woman whose heart had been broken years before could know. Thus, Coquette dwelt in gladness until the day her father returned from his travels with an astonishing tale to tell.

Antoine de Bellamont returned from his travels by way of Roanan bearing a tale of such great adventure to hardly be believed. Further, at the center of Antoine's story loomed a man—the dark Lord of Roanan. Known for his cruel nature, heartlessness, and tendency to violence, the Lord of Roanan had accused Antoine de Bellamont of wrongdoing and demanded recompense. Antoine had promised recompense would be paid— with the hand of his youngest daughter in marriage.

Thus, Coquette found herself lost—thrust onto a dark journey of her own. This journey would find her carried away to Roanan Manor—delivered into the hands of the dark and mysterious Lord of Roanan who dominated it.

The Time of Aspen Falls
Contemporary Romance

Aspen Falls was happy. Her life was good. Blessed with a wonderful family and a loyal best friend—Aspen did know a measure of contentment.

Still, to Aspen it seemed something was missing—something hovering just beyond her reach—something entirely satisfying that would ensure her happiness. Yet, she couldn't consciously determine what the "something" was. And so, Aspen sailed through life—not quite perfectly content perhaps—but grateful for her measure of contentment.

Grateful, that is, until he appeared—the man in the park—the stranger who jogged passed the bench where Aspen sat during her lunch break each day. As handsome as a dream, and twice as alluring, the man epitomized the absolute stereotypical "real man"—and Aspen's measure of contentment vanished!

Would Aspen Falls reclaim the comfortable contentment she once knew? Or would the handsome real-man-stranger linger in her mind like a sweet, tricky venom—poisoning all hope of Aspen's ever finding true happiness with any other man?

Dusty Britches
Historical Romance

Angelina Hunter was seriously minded, and it was

a good thing. Her father's ranch needed a woman who could endure the strenuous work of ranch life. Since her mother's death, Angelina had been that woman. She had no time for frivolity—no time for a less severe side of life. Not when there was so much to be done— hired hands to feed, a widower father to care for, and an often ridiculously light-hearted younger sister to worry about. No. Angelina Hunter had no time for the things most young women her age enjoyed.

And yet, Angelina had not always been so hardened. There had been a time when she boasted a fun, flirtatious nature even more delightful than her sister Becca's—a time when her imagination soared with adventurous, romantic dreams. But that all ended years before at the hand of one man. Her heart turned to stone…safely becoming void of any emotion save impatience and indifference.

Until the day her dreams returned, the day the very maker of her broken heart rode back into her life. As the dust settled from the cattle drive which brought him back, would Angelina's heart be softened? Would she learn to hope again? Would her long-lost dreams become a blessed reality?

The Heavenly Surrender
Historical Romance

Genieva Bankmans had willfully agreed to the arrangement. She had given her word, and she would not dishonor it. But when she saw, for the first time, the man whose advertisement she had answered…

she was desperately intimidated. The handsome and commanding Brevan McLean was not what she had expected. He was not the sort of man she had reconciled herself to marrying.

This man, this stranger whose name Genieva now bore, was strong-willed, quick-tempered, and expectant of much from his new wife. Brevan McLean did not deny he had married her for very practical reasons only. He merely wanted any woman whose hard work would provide him assistance with the brutal demands of farm life.

But Genieva would learn there were far darker things, grave secrets held unspoken by Brevan McLean concerning his family and his land. Genieva Bankmans McLean was to find herself in the midst of treachery, violence, and villainy with her estranged husband deeply entangled in it.

Shackles of Honor
Historical Romance

Cassidy Shea's life was nothing if not serene. Loving parents and a doting brother provided happiness and innocent hope in dreaming as life's experience. Yes, life was blissful at her beloved home of Terrill.

Still, for all its beauty and tranquility…ever there was something intangible and evasive lurking in the shadows. And though Cassidy wasted little worry on it…still she sensed its existence, looming as a menacing fate bent on ruin.

And when one day a dark stranger appeared,

Cassidy could no longer ignore the ominous whispers of the secrets surrounding her. Mason Carlisle, an angry, unpredictable man materialized…and seemingly with Cassidy's black fate at his heels.

Instantly Cassidy found herself thrust into a world completely unknown to her, wandering in a labyrinth of mystery and concealments. Serenity was vanquished… and with it, her dreams.

Or were all the secrets so guardedly kept from Cassidy…were they indeed the cloth, the very flax from which her dreams were spun? From which eternal bliss would be woven?

The Fragrance of Her Name
Historical Romance

Love—the miraculous, eternal bond that binds two souls together. Lauryn Kennsington knew the depth of it. Since the day of her eighth birthday, she had lived the power of true love—witnessed it with her own heart. She had talked with it—learned not even time or death can vanquish it. The Captain taught her these truths—and she loved him all the more for it.

Yet now—as a grown woman—Lauryn's dear Captain's torment became her own. After ten years, Lauryn had not been able to help him find peace— the peace his lonely spirit so desperately needed—the peace he'd sought every moment since his death over fifty years before.

Still, what of her own peace? The time had come. Lauryn's heart longed to do the unthinkable—selfishly abandon her Captain for another—a mortal man who had stolen her heart—become her only desire.

Would Lauryn be able to put tormented spirits to rest and still be true to her own soul? Or, would she have to make a choice—a choice forcing her to sacrifice one true love for another?

An Old-Fashioned Romance
Contemporary Romance

Life went along simply, if not rather monotonously, for Breck McCall. Her job was satisfying, she had true friends. But she felt empty—as if party of her soul was detached and lost to her. She longed for something—something which seemed to be missing.

Yet, there were moments when Breck felt she might almost touch something wonderful. And most of those moments came while in the presence of her handsome, yet seemingly haunted boss—Reese Thatcher.

Romantic Vignettes—The Anthology of Premiere Novellas
Historical Romance
Includes Three Novellas:
The Unobtainable One

Annette Jordan had accepted the unavoidable reality that she must toil as a governess to provide for herself. Thankfully, her charge was a joy—a vision of youthful beauty, owning a spirit of delight.

But it was Annette's employer, Lord Gareth Barrett, who proved to be the trial—for she soon found herself living in the all-too-cliché governess's dream of having fallen desperately in love with the man who provided her wages.

The child loved her—but could she endure watching hopelessly as the beautiful woman from a neighboring property won Lord Barrett's affections?

The General's Ambition

Seemingly overnight, Renee Millings found herself orphaned and married to the indescribably handsome, but ever frowning, Roque Montan. His father, The General, was obsessively determined that his lineage would continue posthaste—with or without consent of his son's new bride.

But when Roque reveals the existence of a sworn oath that will obstruct his father's ambition, will the villainous General conspire to ensure the future of his coveted progeny to be born by Renee himself? Will Renee find the only means of escape from the odious General to be that of his late wife—death? Or will the son find no tolerance for his father's diabolic plotting concerning the woman Roque legally terms his wife?

Indebted Deliverance

Chalyce LaSalle had been grateful to the handsome recluse, Race Trevelian, when he had delivered her from certain tragedy one frigid winter day. He was addictively attractive, powerful, and intriguing—and there was something else about him—an air of secreted internal torture. Yet, as the brutal character of her emancipator began to manifest, Chalyce commenced in wondering whether the fate she now faced would be any less insufferable than the one from which he had delivered her.

Still, his very essence beckoned hers. She was drawn to him and her soul whispered that his mind needed deliverance as desperately as she had needed rescue that cold winter's noon.

The Rogue Knight
Historical Romance

An aristocratic birthright and the luxurious comforts of profound wealth did nothing to comfort Fontaine Pratina following the death of her beloved parents. After two years in the guardianship of her mother's arrogant and selfish sister, Carileena Wetherton, Fontaine's only moments of joy and peace were found in the company of the loyal servants of Pratina Manor. Only in the kitchens and servants' quarters of her grand domicile did Fontaine find friendship, laughter, and affection.

Always, the life of a wealthy orphan destined to inherit loomed before her—a dark cloud of hopeless, shallow, snobbish people…a life of aristocracy, void of simple joys—and of love. Still, it was her lot—her birthright, and she saw no way of escaping it.

One brutal, cold winter's night a battered stranger appeared at the kitchen servants' entrance, however, seeking shelter and help. He gave only his first name, Knight…and suddenly, Fontaine found herself experiencing fleeting moments of joy in life. For

Knight was handsome, powerful…the very stuff of the legends of days of old. Though a servant's class was his, he was proud and strong, and even his name seemed to portray his persona absolutely. He distracted Fontaine from her dull, hopeless existence.

Yet there were devilish secrets—strategies cached by her greedy aunt, and not even the handsome and powerful Knight could save her from them. Or could he? And if he did—would the truth force Fontaine to forfeit her Knight, her heart's desire…the man she loved—in order to survive?

Daydreams
Contemporary Romance

Sayler Christy knew chances were slim to none that any of her silly little daydreams would ever actually come true—especially any daydreams involving Mr. Booker, the new patient—the handsome, older patient convalescing in her grandfather's rehabilitation center.

Yet, working as a candy striper at Rawlings Rehab, Sayler couldn't help but dream of belonging to Mr. Booker—and Mr. Booker stole her heart—perhaps unintentionally—but with very little effort. Gorgeous, older, and entirely unobtainable—Sayler knew Mr. Booker would unknowingly enslave her heart for many years to come—for daydreams were nothing more than a cruel joke inflicted by life. All dreams—daydreams or otherwise—never came true. Did they?

Love Me
Contemporary Romance

Jacey Whittaker couldn't remember a time when she hadn't loved Scott Pendleton—the boy next door. She couldn't remember a time when Scott hadn't been in her life—in her heart. Yet Scott was every other girl's dream too. How could Jacey possibly hope to win such a prize—the attention, the affections, the very heart of such a sought-after young man? Yet win him she did! He became the bliss of her youthful heart—at least for a time.

Still, some dreams live fulfilled—and some are lost. Loss changes the very soul of a being. Jacey wondered if her soul would ever rebound. Certainly, she went on—lived a happy life—if not so full and perfectly happy a life as she once lived. Yet she feared she would never recover—never get over Scott Pendleton—her first love.

Until the day a man walked into her apartment—into her apartment and into her heart. Would this man be the one to heal her broken heart? Would this man be her one true love?

Born for Thorton's Sake
Historical Romance

Maria Castillo Holt…the only daughter of a valiant Lord and his Spanish beauty. Following the tragic deaths of her parents, Maria would find herself spirited away by conniving kindred in an endurance of neglect and misery.

However, rescued at the age of thirteen by Brockton Thorton, the son of her father's devoted friend Lord Richard Thorton, Maria would at last find blessed reprieve. Further Brockton Thorton became, from that day forth, ever the absolute center of Maria's very existence. And as the blessed day of her sixteenth birthday dawned, Maria's dreams of owning her heart's desire seemed to become a blissful reality.

Yet a fiendish plotting intruded, and Maria's hopes of realized dreams were locked away within dark, impenetrable walls. Would Maria's dreams of life with the handsome and coveted Brockton Thorton die at the hands of a demon strength?

Divine Deception
Historical Romance

Mistreated, disheartened, and trapped, Fallon Ashby unexpectedly found the chance of swift deliverance at the hand of a wealthy landowner. The mysterious deliverer offered Fallon escape from unendurable circumstances. Thus, Fallon chose to marry Trader Donavon, a man who concealed his face within the dark shadows of an ominous black hood—a man who unknowingly held her heart captive.

Yet malicious villainy, intent on destroying Trader Donavon, set out to defeat him. Would evil succeed in overpowering the man whose face Fallon had never seen? The ever-hooded hero Fallon silently loved above all else?

Sudden Storms
Historical Romance

Rivers Brighton was a wanderer—having nothing and belonging to no one. Still, by chance, Rivers found herself harboring for a time beneath the roof of the kind-hearted Jolee Gray and her remarkably attractive yet ever-grumbling brother, Paxton. Jolee had taken Rivers in, and Rivers had stayed.

Helplessly drawn to Paxton's alluring presence and unable to escape his astonishing hold over her, however, Rivers knew she was in danger of enduring great heartbreak and pain. Paxton appeared to find Rivers no more interesting than a brief cloudburst. Yet the man's spirit seemed to tether some great and devastating storm—a powerful tempest bridled within, waiting for the moment when it could rage full and free, perhaps destroying everything and everyone in its wake—particularly Rivers.

Could Rivers capture Paxton's attention long enough to make his heart her own? Or would the storm brewing within him destroy her hopes and dreams of belonging to the only man she had ever loved?

The Prairie Prince
Historical Romance

For Katie Matthews, life held no promise of true happiness. Life on the prairie was filled with hard labor, a brutal father, and the knowledge she would need to marry a man incapable of truly loving a woman. Men didn't have time to dote on women—so Katie's father told her. To Katie, it seemed life would forever remain mundane and disappointing—until the day Stover Steele bought her father's south acreage.

Handsome, rugged, and fiercely protective of four orphaned sisters, Stover Steele seemed to have stepped from the pages of some romantic novel. Yet his heroic character and alluring charm only served to remind Katie of what she would never have—true love and happiness the likes found only in fairytales. Furthermore, evil seemed to lurk in the shadows, threatening Katie's brightness, hope, and even her life!

Would Katie Matthews fall prey to disappointment, heartache, and harm? Or could she win the attentions of the handsome Stover Steele long enough to be rescued?

A Better Reason to Fall in Love
Contemporary Romance

"Boom chicka wow wow!" Emmy whispered.

"Absolutely!" Tabby breathed as she watched Jagger Brodie saunter past.

She envied Jocelyn for a moment, knowing he was most likely on his way to drop something off on Jocelyn's desk—or to speak with her. Jocelyn got to talk with Jagger almost every day, whereas Tabby was lucky if he dropped graphics changes off to her once a week.

"Ba boom chicka wow wow!" Emmy whispered again. "He's sporting a red tie today! Ooo! The power tie! He must be feeling confident."

Tabby smiled, amused and yet simultaneously

amazed at Emmy's observation. She'd noticed the red tie, too. "There's a big marketing meeting this afternoon," she told Emmy. "I heard he's presenting some hard-nose material."

"Then that explains it," Emmy said, smiling. "Mr. Brodie's about to rock the company's world!"

"He already rocks mine…every time he walks by," Tabby whispered.

The Tide of the Mermaid Tears
Historical Romance

She took two more steps and paused—squeezed her eyes tightly shut, and Ember gasped as she looked forward up the shore to see a man struggling in the water. He was coughing—spitting water from his mouth as he crawled from the water and onto the sand. As he collapsed facedown on the shore, Ember lifted her skirt and ran toward the man, dropping to her knees beside him.

"Sir?" she cried, nudging one broad shoulder. The man was stripped of his shirt—dressed only in a pair of trousers—no shoes…

Ember shook her head, rolling her eyes at her own foolishness.

"Sir?" she called again, nudging his broad shoulder once more. The man lay on his stomach—his face turned away from her. "Are you dead, sir?" she asked. Placing a hand to his back, she sighed with relief as she felt he yet breathed.

"Sir?" she said, clambering over the man's broad torso.

The man coughed. His eyes opened—his deep blue eyes, so shaded by thick, wet lashes that Ember wondered how it was he could see beyond them.

"Sir?" Ember ventured.

He coughed, asking, "Where am I?"

"On the seashore, sir," Ember answered.

Kiss in the Dark
Contemporary Romance

"Boston," he mumbled.

"I mean…Logan…he's like the man of my dreams! Why would I blow it? What if…" Boston continued to babble.

"Boston," he said. The commanding sound of his voice caused Boston to cease in her prattling and look to him.

"What?" she asked, somewhat grateful he'd interrupted her panic attack.

He frowned and shook his head.

"Shut up," he said. "You're all worked up about nothing." He reached out, slipping one hand beneath her hair to the back of her neck.

Boston was so startled by his touch, she couldn't speak—she could only stare up into his mesmerizing green eyes. His hand was strong and warm, powerful and reassuring.

"If it freaks you out so much…just kiss in the dark," he said.

Boston watched as Vance put the heel of his free hand to the light switch. In an instant the room went black.

The Light of the Lovers' Moon
Historical Romance

Violet Fynne was haunted—haunted by memory. It had been nearly ten years since her father had moved the family from the tiny town of Rattler Rock to the city of Albany, New York. Yet the pain and guilt in Violet's heart were as fresh and as haunting as ever they had been.

It was true Violet had been only a child when her family moved. Still—though she had been unwillingly pulled away from Rattler Rock—pulled away from him she held most dear—her heart had never left—and her mind had never forgotten the promise she had made—a promise to a boy—to a boy she had loved—a boy she had vowed to return to.

Yet the world changes—and people move beyond pain and regret. Thus, when Violet Fynne returned to Rattler Rock, it was to find that death had touched those she had known before—that the world had indeed changed—that unfamiliar faces now intruded on beloved memories.

Had she returned too late? Had Violet Fynne lost her chance for peace—and happiness? Would she be forever haunted by the memory of the boy she had loved nearly ten years before?

Sweet Cherry Ray
Historical Romance

Cherry glanced at her pa, who frowned and slightly shook his head. Still, she couldn't help herself, and she leaned over and looked down the road.

She could see the rider and his horse—a large buckskin stallion. As he rode nearer, she studied his white shirt, black flat-brimmed hat, and double-breasted vest. Ever nearer he rode, and she fancied his pants were almost the same color as his horse, with silver buttons running down the outer leg. Cherry had seen a similar manner of dress before—on the Mexican vaqueros that often worked for her pa in the fall.

"Cherry," her pa scolded in a whisper as the stranger neared them.

She straightened and blushed, embarrassed by being as impolite in her staring as the other town folk were in theirs. It seemed everyone had stopped whatever they had been doing to walk out to the street and watch the stranger ride in.

No one spoke—the only sound was that of the breeze, a falcon's cry overhead and the rhythm of the rider's horse as it slowed to a trot.

Kissing Cousins
Contemporary Romance

"It won't change your life..." he said, his voice low and rich like a warm drink laced with molasses. "And it sure won't be the best kiss you'll ever have," he added. Her body erupted into goose bumps as his thumb traveled slowly over her lower lip. "But I'll try to make it worth your time..."

Take a Walk with Me
Contemporary Romance

"Grandma?" Cozy called as she closed the front door behind her. She inhaled a deep breath—bathing in the warm, inviting scent of banana nut bread baking in the oven. "Grandma? Are you in here?"

"Cozy!" her grandma called in a loud whisper. "I'm in the kitchen. Hurry!"

Cozy frowned—her heart leapt as worry consumed her for a moment. Yet, as she hurried to the kitchen to find her grandma kneeling at the window that faced the new neighbors yard, and peering out with a pair of binoculars, she exhaled a sigh of relief.

"Grandma! You're still spying on him?" she giggled.

"Get down! They'll see us! Get down!" Dottie ordered in a whisper, waving one hand in a gesture that Cozy should duck.

Giggling with amusement at her grandma's latest antics, Cozy dropped to her hands and knees and crawled toward the window.

"Who'll see us?" she asked.

"Here," Dottie whispered, pausing only long enough to reach for a second set of binoculars sitting on the nearby counter. "These are for you." She smiled at Cozy—winked as a grin of mischief spread over her face. "And now...may I present the entertainment for this evening…Mr. Buckly hunk of burning love Bryant…and company."

CPSIA information can be obtained at www.ICGtesting.com
Printed in the USA
242440LV00001B/9/P